THE HOUSE ON CEDAR STREET

STEFON MEARS

Thousand
Faces
Publishing

Also by Stefon Mears

Cavan Oltblood Series
Half a Wizard
The Ice Dagger
Spells of Undeath

Spells for Hire
Devil's Shoestring
Zombie Powder
Spirit Trap
Dragon's Blood (coming December 2019)

The Rise of Magic
Magician's Choice
Sleight of Mind
Lunar Alchemy
Three Fae Monte
The Sphinx Principle

The Telepath Trilogy
Surviving Telepathy
Immoral Telepathy
Targeting Telepathy

Edge of Humanity
Caught Between Monsters
Hunting Monsters

Power City Tales
Not Quite Bulletproof
No Money in Heroism

Devil's Night
Portal-Land, Oregon
Stealing from Pirates
Fade to Gold
With a Broken Sword
Twice Against the Dragon
The House on Cedar Street
Sudden Death
On the Edge of Faerie
Confronting Legends (Spells & Swords Vol. 1)
Uncle Stone Teeth and Other Macabre Poems
The Patreon Collection, Vol. 1-4 (Vol. 5, coming soon)

Published by Thousand Faces Publishing, Portland, Oregon

http://1kfaces.com

ISBN: 978-1-948490-04-7

THE HOUSE ON CEDAR STREET

A Supernatural Thriller

PROLOGUE

Excerpt from 1996 interview with Barclay "Bones" McElroy

Everyone always said the house was haunted. Far back as I can remember, anyway.

Back in the 70s it was owned by a family named Frank. He was a middle manager and she a housewife minding their two-point-three kids. When they moved in, they were the kind of family that kept their lawn grass trimmed to exactly three inches and washed their own windows, even the little ones they needed a ladder to reach above the long, winding staircase next to the front door.

And a big place like that's got a lot of windows.

When they moved out, their lawn was patchy and their windows dirty and every one of the Franks jumped at any change in the wind. In their six months in that house they never did invoke the g-word though, not unless they were talking to someone they really trusted. And even then it was hushed and furtive.

When the Franks ran screaming for the state line, they sold off to a young couple named Jenkins, who thought it looked like a fabulous fixer-upper for a rock bottom price.

They didn't last three weeks.

Didn't talk to anyone before they left, but the neighbors all swore up and down on a stack of bibles that they heard screams coming from that house that didn't sound like they were of the young-couple-trying-to-have-kids variety. Shrill. Painful even. The kind that must have left them hoarse, if it left them with any voice at all.

That was around the time that even the more skeptical neighbors began to have quiet conversations during pauses in trimming the hedges or hanging the laundry. Because not all of the neighbors were of the opinion that the screams came from human throats. And while only a few of the neighbors were saying that at first, well, the ones that weren't were still listening.

The local kids dared each other to open the gate, brave the front yard jungle, and ring the doorbell. Those with the courage swore that someone, or some*thing*, could be heard walking up to the door. And Murphy used to tell me every chance he got how that yellow lab of his couldn't pass that house without growling.

Anyway, after the Jenkins took off for parts unknown, the realtors had a hell of a time moving the place. Sat empty for a better part of a decade before the Dumas family — all eight of them, just like it said in the paper — tried to make a go of it.

That was the one that made national news. Put our little town of Briar, California, on the map.

1

—————

SUNDAY JUNE 11TH, 1989. MOVING DAY.

This house was everything Lex could have asked for.

First, it was big. Two stories, with an attic, modified off of the farmhouse style left-over from when Briar, California, was noted for its almond orchards. Before the town started "growing up" and the orchards moved down closer to the river.

Something like that, anyway. Part of the real estate lady's spiel when she was showing the place. Honestly, Lex was too struck by the house itself to listen too closely.

Spacious master bedroom on the first floor, in the back, with its own bathroom. Six bedrooms upstairs, enough for each of the kids to have their own room. Two bathrooms upstairs, too, and a spare half-bath on the main floor. So many bedrooms and bathrooms that Lex felt as though he'd doubled his salary moving here, even though he'd taken a small pay cut for the opportunity.

And an attic, where Gina could go back to her painting, or that they could make up as a guest room whenever Lex's parents wanted to swing by for a weekend.

Or maybe Gina's parents would even deign to visit them from Jersey. Not that Lex felt any need to encourage them.

Two staircases. One spiral just inside the front door, and a regular set in the back beside the mud room.

An honest-to-God mud room. Lex didn't even know they *made* those in California.

Speaking of things Lex wasn't used to in California, the house had a full, finished basement too. Realtor called it a "rumpus room," which made Lex waggle his eyebrows at Gina. She was more interested in the laundry hook-ups. Enough space for their industrial size washer and dryer.

All-in-all, this one house had more square footage than all of Lex's college dorm rooms and post-college apartments with Gina combined. Including that condo in Sunnyvale that still hadn't sold.

Full acre lot, too, with monkey bars and a swing set that needed nothing but a coat of paint. Lex grew up playing in parks smaller than that backyard. And to have his own almond, orange and lemon trees just inside the redwood fence?

Practically a dream come true.

The yard though, the playset, even the trees, those were all secondary concerns. All that really mattered when Lex and Gina were looking the house over was that it was big and it was only a ten-minute drive down city streets to the factory.

Lex was now in charge of the newest IQ Printer factory, opening at the end of the month. And if he ran it right, one day it could be the biggest. That was the real goal of taking the job. The whole point of moving away from Sunnyvale and uprooting the kids.

God knew Briar had the room to expand.

And if Lex Dumas managed that IQ Printer factory right, built it up, he had a real shot at making the right kind of waves to move up to a C-level post.

In the long run, his family would thank him for "consigning" them to "this little nowhere" as their eldest son, Mason, liked to call it. But Mason was newly eighteen, and off to UCLA in the fall.

Mason didn't get a vote.

Still, Lex had to admit that Mason had a point.

Briar sat in a little, almost forgotten part of California. Not near the megalopolises of L.A. or the Bay Area, nor in what people thought of as proper farm country way to the north or surrounding the highways on the long stretch between megalopolises.

Megalopoli? Lex wasn't sure which was the right plural. He'd just loved the word "megalopolis" since he was a kid. Liked the way it rolled off his tongue.

Either way, Briar was south of Gilroy and east of Monterey. So south of garlic fields and east of a tourist town made famous by its aquarium.

In other words, Briar sat smack in the center of nowhere.

But if this was nowhere, as far as Lex could tell he had the best house in it.

So Lex was laughing and singing bits of *Baba O'Riley* as he drove his family to their new home on moving day. In the back of the mini-van, the kids didn't share his enthusiasm for their new home — or maybe they just weren't crazy about hitting the road at the crack of dawn — but he had every intention of getting them caught up in his excitement.

"Cedar Street," he said, turning right off of Main. "We're almost there, kids. Say, you think they have cedar trees down here too? Bet we could get a good price on cedar chests for storing winter clothes."

Sullen silence from the kids. Like little ghosts in shorts and tee shirts. Not even the twins had said a word since polishing off the breakfast toaster waffles, and usually the twins couldn't go five minutes without talking.

Gina shot him a worried look from the front passenger seat, but Lex only smiled back. Gina was easy to smile at, especially wearing a tank top with her shorts.

"Look at all these trees," he said. Oaks and maples and ashes lined the wide street. Every house had a thick, green lawn. Most of them were one story, but Lex could see a couple that might rival the size of his own house.

He rolled down his window, making a show of inhaling deep that summer air.

"Telling you kids, by the end of the week you'll be loving this place as much as we do, right, Gina?"

Gina missed her cue, either watching a saggy old man holding a frayed red leash, or the saggy old yellow lab at the other end of that leash, watering somebody's begonias.

"Maybe we can get a dog," he said, watching Byron's eyes grow wide in the rear view mirror. Rail skinny and in the middle of a growth spurt, Byron had Lex's sandy blonde hair and Gina's dark hazel eyes. He was thirteen, and he'd been begging for a dog half his life. "No home owners' association here..."

"Let's get *us* settled first," said Gina, over her shoulder to the now-bouncing Byron.

"Time to start then," said Lex, pulling into the double-wide driveway next to the moving truck. His Mercury Sable was already parked along the curb where he'd left it when they finalized the paperwork last week.

"We're here."

GINA WANTED SO BADLY TO LOVE THIS PLACE, BUT SOMETHING ABOUT IT felt too good to be true. All the realty listings in Briar cost no more than half, maybe a third of what the same house would have cost in Sunnyvale, and Sunnyvale was cheap compared to places like Palo Alto or Atherton. But the house on Cedar Street underpriced them all.

When the inspection reports came back clean, Lex had still pushed and offered thousands below the asking price.

The sellers still said yes that very day and wanted to expedite escrow.

Lex just laughed and said he should have offered less. Gina, well, Gina got nervous.

Lex liked to tease Gina about being an Italian girl from New Jersey, mostly because he knew the truth — her family, the Faranettis, never had anything to do with organized crime. But Gina knew other girls growing up. Boys too. Kids who had an "extra" Atari. Or an "extra" Zenith, with remote control. Kids who sold those "extras" — not to Gina, she was a good girl — for much less than the stores were asking.

Growing up around kids like those at St. Vincent's, Gina learned early that if anybody offered too good a deal, something had to be wrong.

And the house looked like too good a deal.

Lex had wanted to sign that day and start the process, but Gina got him to wait a week. She wanted two, but Lex worried the sellers would come to their senses, so she had to settle for one. First she went over all the inspection reports with a fine tooth comb, but the house looked to be in good shape. Gina's own inspector — friend of a cousin who made the move to California decades ago with her Aunt Carmella and Uncle Esteban — said it needed a little work on the drywall, the stairs, and the hardwood floors, but that the bones of the house were sound. And the wiring and pipes were even better.

So it wasn't the house itself then. That meant only one thing.

Gina spent all her free hours that week down at the courthouse and the library, going through recorded documents and microfiches trying to find out who got murdered in that house.

House was built in the late 1960s, and if anybody every got murdered there, the whole town must have covered it up. Not a peep in the papers, and for a flea-speck town like Briar it should have been front page news.

Changed owners pretty fast a few times, and had sat vacant for near on a decade, but that happened sometimes. Especially in a small town. Gina's sister Marie had moved to a small town in Pennsylvania five years back, and she complained sometimes about people who would move in across the street, only to discover they couldn't handle small town life and take off inside of six months.

Gina wasn't sure *she* was cut out for small town life. But what choice did she have? Shoot down Lex's dreams?

She'd die first.

So as Lex pulled the minivan into the driveway that moving day morning, she looked up at the big white house and said, "Isn't it beautiful, kids?"

And it was. Lots of windows, with pistachio green shutters (pure ornamentation) and trim. It even had a white picket fence, just like all the houses she'd dreamed of as a little girl.

"Just look at that huge, wraparound front porch. We could get a nice round table for it, maybe some wicker chairs. Perfect for playing cards, or drinking lemonade with the neighbors. You could do either in the pouring rain and stay bone dry under that roof."

One of the twins — probably Diamanta — grunted. Byron was bouncing up and down, squeaking the poor bench seat something fierce, but Gina knew the boy wasn't thinking about cards or lemonade. Why did Lex have to dangle the promise of a dog so soon? Gina'd wanted to wait a week or three first, try to get them to love the new house before adding to their brood.

Besides, as it was the minivan smelled like French fries and corn chips and sweat and teenage experiments with cologne and perfume. The thought of adding *eau de retriever* to the mix didn't do anything to help settle Gina's stomach.

"And the movers are early," she sallied, pointing at the truck, and the men in white overalls who were manhandling her good brown sectional. "Isn't that great? No sleeping bags tonight!"

Nothing.

Lex pulled on the emergency brake hard enough to jerk the minivan to a stop. Lex had such fine, strong features — rugged brow, solid jawline, strong lips and flashing green eyes. She never liked to see them creased with irritation, like they were now.

He leaned around and spoke in his management voice. "Look..." He must have heard Gina suck in her breath because his nostrils flared and he continued in a calmer voice. "This is our home now, guys. It's not what you're used to, but it's big and it's beautiful, and you'll have all summer to check out the town before school starts. You're all acting like this is the worst thing that ever happened to you. But it can be the *best* thing. You're the one who decides which it is."

If he hadn't gotten out of the minivan right then, Gina might have kissed him. But he was already off to talk to the movers.

Pity. She loved it when he spat out bits of fatherly wisdom like that.

"Your Dad's right, kids," she teased, then got a little more serious herself. "I know you miss your friends. But you'll see. We've got such a big backyard we can invite them all down and for a private campout."

"Really?"

Yes! First score for Gina. That was the shaky voice of little Ava, so pretty with her long black hair, but a tomboy through and through.

"I promise. Fourth of July. Your dad and I already agreed. You can each invite up to three friends, and you can all camp out in the backyard. And I hear they get some pretty big fireworks down here..."

That got most of them moving. No doubt Diamanta was missing her boyfriend, but they were getting too serious for Gina's taste anyway.

Gina got out of the minivan and started ushering her children into their new home.

ELLIOTT DUMAS WASN'T SURE THAT MOVING TO THE ASS-END OF California was the worst thing that ever happened to him. It certainly wasn't the *best*, but the *worst*?

Well, it had a lot of competition.

Competition that started with his name.

Dumas. Should have been a great name, right? Everyone loves *The Three Musketeers*. And it might not have been so bad if they'd pronounced it French-style: doo-MA. But no. Grampa Claude came over at the end of "Double-you Double-you Two" and when the idiots at Ellis Island pronounced his name "DOO-moss" Grampa adopted the pronunciation as a badge of his new country. The whole family was expected to follow suit.

So instead of the other kids turning his surname into something cool like "Doom" for a nickname, Eli had been stuck with either "moss" or "dumbass," depending on whether or not the kid was looking for a fight.

And his first name — Elliott — was beneath contempt. That wasn't even about nicknames, though "Smelliott" had started day one of kindergarten. No, it just sounded ... it sounded like a kind of cheese or something. *We have Brie, Camembert, and Elliott.*

He started going by Eli by the time he was six. Helped that his twin sister Diamanta liked to go by Dee. Eli was much cooler. And it spared him at least a little teasing when that *E.T.* movie came out.

Some, anyway.

A *lot* of competition for the worst thing to happen to Eli in his life.

But as he stood there on the smooth, paved driveway and looked up at the new house, he shoved his lips around his face and tried to decide where this fell on the scale.

Mason was already through the front door, no doubt choosing the best bedroom for himself. As the oldest — by a whole two years over sixteen-year-old Eli and Dee — he no doubt felt it was his right. Not that he'd be using it come September.

Bryon was running around the side of the house, either excited about the backyard campout or the prospect of a dog. Tough to say which. Mom was leading both Ava and Roy by the hand towards the new house, which would irritate Ava who was four years older than six-year-old Roy, and tired of being treated like a child.

Probably be chasing Byron into the back, if Mom let her.

"*Ithika tathika na?*" said Dee, stepping up next to him, dressed in matching jean shorts, but a red tee shirt to contrast Elliot's blue-and-gold Golden State Warriors shirt. That meant *What do you think?* in their personal twinspeak, the language they developed between themselves when they were little.

She must have felt nervous. They hardly used their personal language these days, and never where their parents could hear. Some child psychologist had called the language a "developmental phase" that would pass, and if Mom and Dad heard it now Eli and Dee might find themselves seeing a shrink again.

They couldn't give it up, though. It was something they shared that no one else did. Proof that Eli and Dee were closer than any other brothers or sisters could understand.

In fact, in quiet moments, inside his own head and nowhere else, Eli would admit that Dee was part of the reason he hated the name "Elliott." He already had an effeminate reflection of himself running around. He didn't need an effeminate name too.

Not that he'd ever admit *that* out loud, either. His parents could be sensitive about that kind of thing. Mason once complained about being named after a bricklayer and got a two-hour lecture on names, jobs, and family history. With homework.

Hard to sympathize with Mason. The golden boy. Top grades and top athlete. Scholarship offers from six different universities. Dad's rugged looks and Mom's black hair and eyes. Eli had once heard girls in the school hallway *literally sigh* when Mason walked by.

Mason never even had a pimple.

Eli, like Dee, was only just getting past pimples and praying they didn't come back.

Dee was five-six, just like Eli, making both of them six inches shorter than their dad and their big brother. People called Dee "willowy," and Eli "slender," but Eli just thought of them both as skinny. Muscled though. Dee from her dance and soccer and gymnastics, Eli from swimming and basketball — self-defense choices, since Mason was all-everything at both baseball and football.

Not worth trying to follow in those shoes.

They both had Dad's sandy blonde hair and green eyes too. Dee's hair down past her shoulders and Eli's trimmed short enough to fit comfortably under a swim cap.

But Dee had asked him a question. What did Eli think? He thought it smelled like fresh-cut grass and flowers. He thought he could hear neighbors mowing their lawns a couple of blocks away, but more important he could have sworn he heard the sound of basketball meeting a chain-link, outdoor net.

One of the true sounds of civilization.

He thought it was too warm for ten a.m., and that it might hit the high eighties before the sun set. He thought they were a long way from home, and he had no idea how they could possibly adapt to this town so distant and alien to the place they'd lived their whole life.

He thought they probably couldn't get decent Chinese food here. Or cable television, which meant no ESPN. He thought this was a big old mistake, and that the move would probably rank toward the top of the list of The Worst Things Ever to Happen to Elliot Dumas.

But he couldn't say any of that. He was a whole ninety-three seconds older than Dee, and that meant it was up to him to be strong for her. To protect her.

"*Katha atha neeska nish,*" Eli said, shaking his head. *Not sure yet. Better see inside.*

Dee tilted her head. Didn't need words to say *You first.*

Eli started toward the house.

The lawn was nice and thick. Mason's job to mow until fall, then probably Eli's. Of course. Tall redwood fence between this house — home, he needed to start thinking of it as home whether he liked it or not — and the new neighbors. But not tall enough.

Eli could see some old couple staring from their kitchen window. Eyes narrowed like the Manson family just moved into the center of the block. Chocolate brown skin to go with their gray hair, which was cool. Eli nodded that direction and heard Dee let out the same breath he'd been holding.

They'd both been scared that this was going to be some kind of all-white rural town, the kind that had confederate flags or KKK rallies or something, and all voted so far right that they considered Republicans commies.

But if there was a black family next door, this little berg might at least be integrated.

Might not be so bad. Maybe there'd even be decent Chinese food.

"Lavender?" said Eli as they made their way up the red stone walk toward the front door. He was talking about the flowers and bushes running along the porch, mentioning the only one he thought he recognized.

"And begonias — those are the red, white, and yellow flowers — and Queen Anne's lace," said Dee.

Three steps up to the front porch. The steps creaked. Eli and Dee exchanged a nod. When sneaking out or in they'd jump the steps.

"Hurry up, you two," said Mom through one of the living room windows. Looked like she meant to open all of them. "Your father and I have already tagged your rooms."

"We don't get to choose?" said Dee, as though Mom had just told her she wouldn't get a new dress for prom.

"We were fair and even-handed," said Mom, closing the window again.

Eli and Dee looked at each other.

They raced inside and clanged up the spiral staircase.

———

THE SPIRAL STAIRCASE WAS TOO COOL FOR WORDS. WROUGHT IRON, AND the way it bonged under her sneaks — and Eli's — made Dee smile. The staircase was all wrong for this place, but in all the right ways.

Dee stopped halfway up, letting Eli go the rest of the way without her. Didn't matter. If he saw, or felt, anything supercool she'd know it the minute he did. Always worked that way. For both of them.

Heck, she was half-surprised that Eli hadn't stopped on the stairs when she did, but when she thought about it, she knew why. He knew it was a romance novel thing. Probably put on a burst of speed to get away from it. Preferring the noise and bustle of the movers upstairs.

Dee recognized the new house as farmhouse style at once. Not just the rectangular build and the peaked roof, but the big porch? And the visible beams and hardwood floors on the inside? Practically screamed quaint farmhouse, despite the size. It even smelled of wood oil and dust, strong enough that she popped a stick of wintergreen gum in her mouth before the house tastes settled in her mouth.

But a *wrought iron spiral staircase*? That didn't belong in a farmhouse. That belonged in a mansion or something. And since it wasn't like Mom and Dad were going to hire some farmhand with lots of muscles and tanned skin who could save Dee from wolves or evil landlords or something, thinking of this new house as a kind of mansion was way cooler than letting it stay a farmhouse in her head.

Dee'd have to draw it. The whole place. From a bunch of different angles. Really learn it that way. Really get a strong sense of the place in her head, in a way that would let it be whatever she wanted.

Like Dad was saying. She could choose for this to be the best thing to ever happen to her, and that was much better than letting it be the worst.

Eli would let it be the worst, if she let him. Always grading things on a scale of how good or bad they were in his life. Well, a move could be a change, and maybe she'd help him find a way past that.

Find a way for this move to be awesome for both of them.

Much better than moping over Sebastian. She was going to break up with him anyway. She was sure of it. Even if the move came before she was ready to do it. Sebastian was getting that look a little too often. Like he wanted to move beyond hand stuff, and Dee wasn't sure he was the right guy for that.

But a town like this. Had to have big, strapping farm boys, right? Ones taught by their mommas to respect good girls?

Dee climbed a few steps higher and looked out the window — the one high up the front wall, that was only really a viewing window from two-thirds the way up the stairs. Little blue cottage across the street, like something out of a picture book. Sky blue paint with white trim. Lawn as perfect as the rest of the neighborhood. Garden of daisies under the front windows.

And a big old guy staring straight back at her from the lawn chair on his front porch. Big guy, solid and creepy.

Dee hurried up the last few stairs, but couldn't get the image of the guy out of her head. Looked taller than Dad, and even broader through the shoulders. Had that steel gray hair, combed straight back with a pomp like it was still 1956.

Dee read a couple of old romances about greasers in 1956, bad boys with hearts of gold who just needed the right girl to turn them around. Like Danny Zuko in *Grease*. This guy across the street was no Danny Zuko.

This guy was creepy. Just staring like that. Not smiling. Not waving.

Dee shivered. Forced herself to look around the house. Movers just got Roy's race car bed up the back stairs and were heading down the hall towards her. She ducked into the bathroom beside the stairs to get out of the way.

Smelled nice in here. Open window bringing in the scent of the begonias on a cool breeze for a fairly warm morning. Pale blue tile everywhere, and two — *two* — sinks under a wide mirror. The sink counter was blue tile too, but the mirror was more than enough to make up for it. Wider than her outstretched arms and reaching most of the way to the ceiling.

The old mirror in the kids' bathroom back in Sunnyvale would have fit into this new one at least eight times over.

Dee flipped on the lights and leaned in close for a pimple check.

Still clear.

She knocked on the white cabinet doors below the sink, for luck. Lots of cabinet space in this bathroom too, which was good because she couldn't spot a real medicine cabinet anywhere.

Mom was probably already on top of that though. Probably ready to buy each kid their personal under-sink organizer. Mom was good that way.

The shower stall just inside the door was a bit cramped. Not ideal. But...

Look. At. That. *TUB.*

The bathtub was double-wide and extra-long. Even Mason could probably have used it — not that he would have. It had little claw feet, and separate taps for hot and cold water.

It was glorious.

Dee was half-tempted to strip off and jump in right now. But she had a feeling that would be the wrong—

"What?" said Eli, poking his head around the corner. "What's so..."

Dee looked at him, and knew she had her isn't-it-dreamy expression.

"It's not the tub, is it?" Eli quirked a smile. "Tell me it's not the tub."

"I've always wanted a tub like this." She knelt beside it and ran her hand along the rim. "Like a princess."

Eli shook his head. Got his big-brother tone going.

"Right. Roy's straight across the hall from here, on the other side of the spiral staircase. I'm next to Roy, and Byron's on my other side, then the other upstairs bathroom. Ava's in the room next to this one, then you, then Mason."

"So we're in the middle."

"As always, but I think our rooms may be as big as Mason's."

Dee smirked. "Bet he's not loving that little detail."

"He's got more closet space."

"It's just not fair." Dee got to her feet. "Like a boy knows what to do with closet space. No offense."

"None taken."

Their little joke. She always listened to him bitching about girls and he listened to her bitching about boys. They always ended by saying "no offense" and "none taken" but they both knew they were the exceptions to every rule.

"One more thing," said Eli, and she didn't like the hesitation in his voice. Gave him the wide-eyed I'm-listening look until he continued. "The trap door to the attic? It's between our rooms."

Eli led her to the bathroom doorway and pointed. The trapdoor was down, and Dad was leading two massive, box-carrying movers up a set of squeaking, rickety-looking stairs and into the attic.

So the trap door was between their rooms.

Why did that bother Eli?

LEX SNEEZED OUT DUST. GINA WAS RIGHT. THEY'D HAVE TO AIR OUT this attic for days before they could consider bringing in furniture. If they went the guest room direction. Gina was pushing for that, but wouldn't it be a waste of the big, south-facing windows in the back?

How could she not want to turn at least part of this big attic into a studio? Not like there wasn't room for that *and* a guest room, if that was what she wanted. Still have storage room aplenty left over. The attic was even cooler than the rest of the house, which had to be good for her paints, right?

"Where for these boxes?" That was Hank Giamatti, chief mover. Something like Gina's third cousin, twice removed if Lex remembered right. He couldn't believe sometimes just how big her family was.

Or she was pulling his leg. Hank looked less like Gina than Lex did, with his stocky build and deep, deep tan. Gina barely had a kiss of the olive skin tone her Sicilian father had, getting more of her mother's northern, pale skin.

Lex gave the attic a quick scan and pointed to a spot along the east wall, under the peak of the roof.

"There for now. We'll figure out the rest later."

Hank nodded, and he and his man set down their boxes and went back down for more.

Lex stayed behind and gave the attic a better look. He hadn't noticed much more than the big southern-facing windows last time. It was so much less important than what the house had on the lower levels. Heck, just getting an attic at all was a bonus as far as he was concerned.

Now he needed to know exactly what he had to work with.

The flooring was cherry wood, same as the downstairs. Yellowed a bit, but still pinkish. Rawer up here too, like it wasn't bought in bulk at some warehouse store, but cut from local timber. How cool would that be? Maybe the beams of the house were of the same wood. He'd have to check.

Walls came up a good five feet from the floor before they began to slope toward the peak. So a little tight around the edges, but more than twice Lex's height here in the center of the room. Little windows in the north wall for cross wind.

Lex trotted over and opened them. The one on the right stuck, but gave with a little shoving. The two big windows in the south wall didn't open, but they had two smaller windows flanking them that did. Good enough for a cross breeze. Get out the dust and ... and...

What was that other smell?

Some of it was cleanser. Some of it was oil soap. But underneath that — and the dust — something else. Something ... musky?

Didn't look as though a family of raccoons had moved in up here, but raccoons were all Lex could think of for the smell.

Oh, well. Wouldn't matter once the place had been aired out and Gina got the kids to give it a good cleaning. Speaking of kids, the way Byron was running around the back yard, you'd think he already had a dog running alongside him.

Huh. When Lex was Byron's age, he'd already have climbed the playset and gotten started on the swings. Byron was too busy running to bother with either yet.

In fact, he better come in or he'll be too tired to start unpacking...

Long, slow whistle of admiration from the staircase.

Lex turned to see his eldest, eyes wide and giving the attic the once-over. He was wearing a cut-off jersey to show off his abs while his shorts showed off his legs. More confidence than Lex had at that age, but Lex had never been much of an athlete.

"How 'bout I call *this* room?" said Mason, wonder in his voice.

"You don't get to *call* any room. Your mom and I already decided who gets which room. Be glad you're beside the stairs and the bathroom."

"I am." Mason held up his hands in surrender. "Still. Criminal, throwing this sweet setup away as storage. It's even cooler than the rest of the house. Shouldn't it be hotter?"

"I'll remind you about that storage crack in a few years," said Lex, arching one eyebrow. "You know, when you expect us to keep stuff in storage for you because you don't have room in your apartment."

Mason ignored the jibe and joined his father by the south windows. He gave another whistle. "Who's she?"

Lex followed Mason's gaze. Yellow bikini-clad girl sunbathing next door, with smooth chocolate skin and a face-framing Jheri curl.

He rumpled his son's hair. "And you said this town was too small for good-looking girls."

"I take it back. Now if you'll excuse me, I think I should be a good neighbor and—"

"And start settling into your room," said Lex in a firm voice. "You'll have your bed made and your clothes put away before you consider doing anything 'neighborly,' and if your bed and chest of drawers aren't in your room yet, you'll go help your mother arrange her kitchen."

"Yes, sir," Mason said with a sigh, trudging toward the stairs as only a teenager can.

Lex waited until Mason was three steps down the stairs before getting his attention.

"Oh, and Mase? You're too young to remember this from the last time, but your mother often likes to bake cookies for the neighbors when we move into someplace new. No reason it can't be you delivering them, so long as you come right home afterwards."

The smile on Mason's face was almost enough to make Lex wish he were a kid again.

"Yes, sir!"

"I mean it though. You'll come right back home or you'll spend your first week here grounded. We're eating as a family tonight."

"Yes, sir." Mason even saluted before hustling down the stairs in that quick-step style he favored.

"And call Byron in from outside," Lex called loudly. "He needs to get started unpacking too."

Lex was pretty sure the muffled reply was a yes-sir. He could always count on Mason to do the right thing, when there was a reward waiting at the end of it.

Yes, this new house was going to work out just fine.

Lex spared a glance for the sunbathing beauty next door before he started back for the stairs. At least one of his kids should be happier about the move now...

———

SOMETHING ALWAYS WENT WRONG IN A MOVE. AS FAR BACK AS GINA could remember, she never once had a move that went perfectly smooth. The first time was when she was four, and her Raggedy Ann doll got lost.

Her actual Raggedy Ann. Family heirloom and all that, but more importantly her favorite toy. The one she carried everywhere.

Gina got the blame for the loss. As though she could possibly have set it down and forgotten it. She'd have had as easy a time forgetting to bring her own hands.

No, Gina was sure then — and that sureness had never faded — that her big brother Mike had put it on the roof of the station wagon when he helped her into the back.

Gina could never prove it, but she'd never quite forgiven Mike for the loss.

So far — and here Gina knocked on the fine white oak of her kitchen cabinets as she'd already done a dozen times that day, each time the thought had occurred to her — this move had been smooth.

Everything seemed to be here. Lex had counted the boxes in the bedroom, living room, basement and den. The kids had reported all boxes present in their rooms. Gina herself had gone over the kitchen boxes twice, laid out as they were on the ubiquitous hardwood floor here. Same wood — cherry was it? — for the counters, but not the cabinets. Gina would have bet that the woman of the house insisted on a different kind of wood there, if only to break the monotony and save her sanity.

Speaking of sanity, the kids had started perking up now that they had their own rooms to themselves. (And Byron was still over the moon about even the possibility of a dog, thank you very much, Lex.)

Only one thing had gone wrong so far. Gina hadn't gotten to cook their first meal.

That was a problem. For generations, Faranetti women had always cooked a meal the first night in their new homes. Yes, it started back when the family didn't have much money, and cooking at home was a three-hundred-sixty-five-and-a-quarter-days-a-year thing.

But now, it was a tradition. And it was good luck.

Gina had managed it in the dorm rooms in college, and later her apartments with Lex, and later still their progressively larger condos.

Now, tonight, here she was unpacking Chinese delivery boxes. Cashew chicken and beef with broccoli and sweet and sour pork, with more rice and eggrolls than she knew what to do with.

A good-looking meal, and if it was tasty it would help cement Eli as her ally in spinning the move well.

But she hadn't made it herself.

Not because she didn't have food to cook. She'd brought down chicken and veggies in a cooler just for that purpose. But the gas wasn't on yet, so the oven was a no-go. Lex had spent an hour on the phone with the utility people, but the soonest they could get the gas turned on was tomorrow morning.

In the meantime, that meant cold showers and no stove or oven.

Gina tried not to say anything.

While she was busy sorting the food, Lex was busy organizing the kids (with their paper plates, paper napkins and plastic silverware) around their two-leaf dining room table. It was thin. It was redwood. And it always smelled like crayons no matter what Gina did to clean it. Still, it could sit the entire family, which was no small feat. And if fit perfectly in front of the big, bay, dining room windows. Gave the new neighbors a good look at the newest members of the block and let them see a happy family. Lex at one end, Gina at the other. The two oldest boys on either side of their father, and the two youngest down beside Gina where she could keep them from getting distracted or ... creative.

But Lex must have caught her sighing.

"You *did* prepare the first meal we ate," he said softly when she called the troops into the kitchen to fill their plates. She loved it when he spoke in her ear like that. Even when he was wrong.

"How do you figure?" She gave him the side-eye and brushed her long, black hair over her shoulder. She caught his eyes following the movement and dancing along her bare shoulder. She'd have to wear tank tops more often. "Think I whipped that up with more than the phone on the wall?"

"Remember the P.B. and J's we ate back around noon? Counts as a meal. And you made it."

"One," she said holding up a finger as the kids started shuffling back to their places at the table, "that's not cooking, and two," — she held up a second finger — "you helped make the sandwiches."

"So, what, it's bad luck to have a helpful husband?"

Lex joined the food line before Gina could think of a comeback, but he let her take her proper place in front of him anyway. Reverse age order when they ate buffet style. The surest way to see to it that the little ones got their share before the bottomless pits — Mason and Eli — reached the food.

And with their mother right behind them in line, those two made sure to leave food for her and Lex.

Then they were all sitting around the table, one big family. The kids even sounded excited about the prospect of checking out the neighborhood as they passed around a two-liter of store-brand diet cola. And Mason was certainly eager to distribute cookies — though her first batch of neighbor cookies would have to wait for tomorrow and the gas.

Lex got all their attention for a prayer, which made her smile as they all joined hands. Prayer before dinner was a rare thing in the Dumas household, but Gina was raised a good Catholic girl, and honestly she missed it sometimes.

Lex either knew that, or he knew she needed a little pick-me-up because of the delivery dinner. Or maybe he was just trying to counter the bad luck.

Whatever it was, Gina was glad. And if she hadn't already planned to see about christening the house properly later that night, she'd be planning it now. After they got the kids to bed.

"Heavenly Father," said Lex, "we thank Thee for this food and for all Thy blessings in Jesus' name. Amen."

As Gina picked at bits of broccoli with her chopsticks, she

wondered how Lex would feel about having a priest come bless the house. True, Gina wasn't much of a Catholic these days, but this was a real house, not just another condo.

Didn't it need something special to mark it as theirs?

———

ELI WAS EXHAUSTED BY THE TIME HIS HEAD HIT THE PILLOW THAT NIGHT. Didn't see why, really, but he was. Couldn't have been that much trouble coming up and down the stairs a few dozen times, much less shoving furniture around his room and putting away clothes and trophies.

All right, arranging his room had taken some time. Had his bed under the window, facing the door. Dee had done the same, so when their doors were open, they could see each other across the wood-paneled hall.

At least the walls of the bedrooms were white.

Bureau against one wall next to the closet. Bookshelves on the opposite wall. Desk against the final wall, not that it was much of a desk. More like a half-table with two drawers. Serious study had to be done at the dinner table.

Warriors posters — and Michael Jordan, of course — all over the walls. Plus that Lita Ford poster, the one that always made Mom raise an eyebrow when she saw it, no matter how many times he pointed out that she might not actually be naked, what with the guitar covering her anyway.

Mom didn't object to the *Sports Illustrated* swimsuit calendars Eli and Mason had — or Mason's Heather Thomas poster — but for some reason the Lita Ford poster bugged her. Maybe she blamed it for Eli's wanting a guitar.

The guitar was still "under discussion" between Mom and Dad, which meant it probably wasn't happening.

Anyway, the posters and calendar were up, and the clothes were away in the bureau or the closet. And Eli's basketball and swimming trophies — team trophies, not individual awards like Mason was always winning — along the top shelves of his twin bookcases.

The books and stuff could wait until tomorrow or the next day. Priorities, you know. Mom insisted on lights-out at ten that first night, without even giving a good explanation. Despite the fact that Eli, Dee and Mason usually got to stay up 'til midnight during summer vacations.

Just as well. Eli was ready to sleep.

Zonked straight out practically the moment his head hit the pillow.

So why was he awake right now?

Little red digits on his alarm clock said one twenty-seven.

Then he heard it. A creak. Right above him. Like a footstep in the attic.

Eli shivered. Pulled up the blue electric blanket he'd thrown off earlier.

Silly. Just the house. There wasn't—

Another.

And another.

Someone was up there. Someone was walking over to the trap door.

Eli sat up. Across the hall, Dee was staring right back at him, eyes as wide as his own in the pale moonlight. As one they waited with bated breath for the trap door to open. It had to be Dad, up there for a box that got put in the wrong place or something.

No. Couldn't be Dad. If it were Dad, the trap door would already ... be ... down.

Why was someone up there with the trap door shut?

The footsteps stopped at the trap door. Eli couldn't breathe. He listened so intently he could hear the blood rush past his ears as his heart pounded. Some stranger was up there.

The steps moved away from the door, to Eli's right. Toward the back of the house. Was that how they got in? Through a back window?

Dee zipped across the hall in her baby blue nightgown and jumped into bed next to Eli.

"It's Dad, right?" said Eli. "Has to be Dad."

"Not Dad. He and Mom just finished doing it."

"Eww," said Eli. "Why do you know that?"

"How did you not hear her?" Dee shook her head. "The steps have stopped again."

"I'm going up," said Eli. He started getting out of bed, but Dee grabbed his shoulder.

"*Uthi natika*," she said. *That's stupid.*

"*Jassika inda Mas.*" *Then I'll grab Mason.*

Dee nodded, and huddled under Eli's covers as he got up, wearing nothing but his purple pajama bottoms.

He eased out of the doorway — back to the wood paneling, just in case — then zipped across the hall to Mason's room. Mason's door was shut, of course. Eli tried the handle...

He locked it? First night in a new house and Mason locked his door?

Eli stared at the door. Mom had left a three-by-five card tacked up high in the center, with Mason's name written in red marker. Same as she'd done for everyone to designate the rooms. Mom had a master key for all the bedrooms, but that didn't do Eli much good.

Did Eli dare knock? He was practically underneath whoever was in the attic. They might hear him. But Mason could sleep like the dead. A soft knock wouldn't wake him.

Eli gritted his teeth while his stomach turned flip-flops. Maybe he should just run downstairs and get Dad. If Dee was right, he'd still be awake.

Or maybe he'd be clunked out dead to the world. Wasn't that how it was supposed to work? A guy has sex then has to roll over and go to sleep? Maybe Mason would know, but whatever Mason knew or didn't know was there with him on the other side of that locked door.

Eli ran back to his room.

"Mason's locked the door," he said, sitting on the bed next to Dee. "What do you think?"

"I haven't heard the steps move since you left the room."

"Me either."

"Probably just the house settling. Or raccoons maybe. Dad said something about smelling raccoons up their earlier."

"Probably just that."

Eli didn't believe it for a minute. A few creaks might have been the house settling, but those were footsteps. At least a dozen of them. And raccoons? No reason to think they'd sound like human footsteps.

Someone had to be up there. If that someone hadn't just snuck out the same way they snuck in. Maybe through a back window...

Dee's eyes didn't leave the ceiling. She looked even more scared than Eli felt. Her jaw was moving like her teeth would chatter if she wasn't careful. And she was shaking like it was even colder than it was.

Eli knew what he had to do.

"*Sufina atama as?*" *Do you want to sleep here?*

Dee nodded.

"Right back," said Eli, quick-stepping to the doorway.

Gritting his teeth, and trying to keep each puffed breath silent, he slid down the hall. Back to the pale wood paneling. Byron's door was closed, but not locked.

Eli eased it open. Slowly. So slow—

Creak.

Eli squeezed his eyes tight. Struggled to keep his shaking knees still.

Nothing. No response from above, and no awkward question from Byron.

Eli slipped his hand through the door, turned the lock, and closed the door again. Checked the knob. Wouldn't turn.

One down.

Back down the hall, slow and steady, back past his room toward Roy's. Every muffled step took ages. Eli's ears strained for any sound from above. Any hint that the intruder was moving again.

He heard nothing outside his body. Maybe a breeze in the trees outside. He didn't smell any raccoons either, just wood and oil soap.

Roy's door was open. Eli eased it closed and locked it.

Quick past the spiral staircase. Shivering through a wave of cold as the moonlight hit him through the high window above the wrought iron.

Was that another footstep?

Eli froze. Strained.

Something was wrong. He was sure of it. But he couldn't tell what. Almost like he was being watched. He almost felt like ... almost felt like the intruder in the attic was listening to *him*. For *his* footsteps. But that was ridiculous. Eli's learned to sneak past *Mason* years ago, and Mason could hear the television hum even after it was turned off.

Eli hunched his shoulders up to protect his neck and rushed to Ava's room. Closed and locked the open door.

He wanted to zip back across the hall at fast-break speed, but no. He couldn't shake that being-watched feeling. He needed to be extra quiet right now. Getting-home-with-a-bad-report-card quiet.

Eli's feet knew what to do, arching, rising, lowering, easing down. One after the other. Step by step.

Fortunately the hall wasn't *that* wide.

Eli entered his room and closed the door quietly. And locked it.

Eli crawled back under the covers next to Dee, and the two huddled together until sleep returned.

Sleep was a long time coming.

INTERVIEW SNIPPET

Excerpt from 1996 interview with Barclay "Bones" McElroy

No, we didn't have some kind of betting pool about the Dumas family. I don't know who started that rumor but it's a damn lie. We're decent, God-fearing folks in Briar, no matter what some New York writer says about us.

Truth is, I think most of us were pulling for the poor kids. Eight of 'em in that house, well, that's a lot of love, right? I mean, the Jenkins didn't have any kids yet, and the Franks had only a couple. But eight Dumas? That had to mean something, didn't it?

So, yeah, I'll admit that I was standing vigil that first night. Far as I knew nothing had ever happened to a family on its first night there, but I don't know how these things work. I've never had to live through it myself, thank the Man Upstairs. But I didn't catch a wink of sleep that night for worry over them. Started on my porch while they moved in, then on into my dining room as the hours wore on.

But I didn't see or hear nothing that first night. Yeah, I know Murphy says he did. Says his old yellow lab started growling 'long about one Ack Emma. But Murphy says lots of things, just as long as people are willing to listen.

I'm telling you I was right across the street and I didn't hear nor see anything odd that night.

Well, now, if I heard any of *those* kinds of noises I wouldn't have paid them no mind, and shame on you for asking. Six kids that couple had. Just how exactly did you think they got 'em?

And no, I didn't go over and introduce myself that first day. I don't think any of us did. Not out of fear of the house, just because that couple had their hands full as it was. Orchestrating a move like that. I think we all wanted to give them a little room to maneuver that first day.

All right. Maybe a little of it was fear of that house.

I was living right where I am right now when the Jenkins and the Franks had their turns over there. Not saying there's anything to these rumors of the g-word or anything like that. Just saying, well...

Fine. The place gave me the heebie-jeebies, all right?

Still does.

2

____

MONDAY JUNE 12TH, 1989. DAY ONE.

"Hang back, you two," said Gina.

The morning breakfast was done — scrambled eggs and bacon, thanks to the gas company connecting them first thing this morning. That helped Gina feel a little better, with an actual cooked meal in the new house under her belt, and in the bellies of her family. Especially since Lex had to head out first thing to see about something at the new factory.

Not yet eight-thirty, their first morning in the new house, and Lex was off at work already.

He promised he'd be back by noon though.

He'd better be. Gina wasn't handling all the unpacking herself.

Now Mason was orchestrating kitchen clean-up, which meant using his reach to put the pans back on the copper hanging rack — a rack he had to duck under when he crossed the kitchen — after Byron finished scrubbing them and Ava finished drying them, while Roy got to put the glasses and dishes in the dishwasher.

That dishwasher had to be replaced. It looked horrible. An avocado-green relic of the late 60s or early 70s. Gina just prayed that it still worked.

Only half the kitchen unpacked, but at least the daily use dish-ware and flatware was done. And if the pots and pans came out of boxes as she needed them, at least Mason was good enough to make sure they got put away where she wanted them.

She was going to miss him when he went off to UCLA, but this was not the time to think about her firstborn baby boy running away to college.

She had these two to deal with right now.

Eli and Dee were sitting side-by-side in the center of the dining room table, backs to the front window. They looked exhausted in the warm morning sunshine, pasty and puffy. Her still in her baby blue nightgown, and him in those purple pajama bottoms he loved so much. Gina herself had on old, faded jeans and a light pink blouse.

They were sitting shoulder-to-shoulder, the way they did when they were little and they were scared of a storm or something.

Of course, given the story they'd told her before breakfast, she could understand why they felt scared. But that didn't excuse any of it.

"I don't want you doing that again," said Gina, addressing both twins with the same pronoun. The psychologists had warned her that was a bad habit, that she needed to emphasize their individuality, but they made it so difficult sometimes. "Any of it."

Eli looked like he was going to object, but Dee jostled him before he finished opening his mouth.

"I'm sure those sounds were a little scary, but use your heads. It was just the pipes or something."

"Sounded like footsteps to us," muttered Eli.

"And you say that from the vantage point of long experience in this house?"

She tried leaning forward on the table and giving them a big smile. Anything to make them see how silly they were being. But all she got were uncertain glances.

"Look, it's a big old house, and it's going to have all its own secrets and noises."

"Secrets?" said Dee.

"Sure. Like which steps are good, and which ones will give you away when you're sneaking out." Gina winked at them. "But there wasn't anyone in the attic last night. The front door was locked, and so was the kitchen. I checked them both twice myself before bed. And your father made sure the ground floor windows were shut tight. And you said yourselves that the trap door was shut. We did not have an intruder."

She raised her eyebrows, daring them to contradict her.

"You're sure?" Dee, at least, sounded ready to believe. Good. Time to move on.

"Positive." Gina stood tall and folded her arms under her breasts. "Now in the future, if you think you hear footsteps, I want you to come get your father. Let him deal with it. I don't want you two locking the little ones in their rooms like that."

"Yes, Mom," they said in perfect unison.

Gina flared a sigh through her nose.

"Which brings us to the last thing. You two are sixteen now. You're too old to be sharing a bed."

Dee furrowed her brow as though she couldn't imagine why it might be a problem. Even Eli looked stumped. That was a relief, at least. Gina had been fairly sure nothing would happen between them, but still...

"I know you're twins, but you're still a boy and a girl, and you're both developing."

"*Eww!*"

There was the synchronized disgust Gina'd been waiting for.

"Exactly. And your grandmother would tan your hides — and mine — if she found you two sleeping in the same bed. You're not children anymore. You're young adults, and you need to respect that. You need to sleep in your own beds."

"We were scared," said Dee, leaning harder against her brother.

"And what would Sebastian say? Hmm? What would he say if he'd come to visit and ran up the stairs to find you in bed with your own brother? Behind a locked door yet?"

"Come on, Mom," said Eli. "You're being gross."

Gina sighed again. "*You* know there's nothing sexual about it. *I* know there's nothing sexual about it." Gina resisted the urge to knock on wood. Those two were just *so close*. "But the rest of the world, well, you can't expect *them* to understand. So we have to be safe. Don't we?"

"I thought we weren't supposed to care what other people think," said Dee.

"It's one thing if another girl doesn't like your taste in clothes. This is something else entirely."

They didn't say anything, so Gina brought out the big gun.

"This is important, kids. And if you can't promise me it will stop, well, then we may have to talk to Dr. Clyburn about it."

"Dr. Clyburn's way up in Palo Alto," said Eli.

"She means a phone conference or something," said Dee.

"Whatever it takes," said Gina.

"All right, Mom," said Eli.

"I'm sorry, Mom," said Dee.

"Good." Gina nodded. "I'm glad that's settled. Now Eli, get back to unpacking your room. Dee, come give me a hand with the kitchen."

One attempt to split them up and just like that they were back in unison.

"But, Mom!"

"You can go exploring later this afternoon. I have no intention of living out of boxes for the next ten years, so let's get cracking."

WHY WERE BOOKS HARDER TO PUT AWAY THAN CLOTHES?

Clothes had been nothing to put away. Open the boxes, upend them over the right drawer. Close the drawer and open the next box. Repeat as needed.

CDs had been easy too. Eli always kept his CDs in strict alphabetical-chronological order. Alphabetical by band, and for each band chronological by album. From Accept to Yngwie Malmsteen — correction, Yngwie *J*. Malmsteen, as he insisted on his album covers, no doubt to differentiate the guitar virtuoso from all the other Yngwie Malmsteens out there.

Mason *hated* that Eli filed Yngwie J. Malmsteen under Y instead of under M, but Eli didn't care. After all, neither Eli nor any of his friends had ever said, "Put on some Malmsteen" or "some Roth." It was always, "Let's hear some Yngwie!" or "Crank up the David Lee."

As far as Eli was concerned, an artist's name might as well be a title.

And putting the CDs away had been fun. First thing he'd done after unpacking his stereo. Well, what he called his stereo, anyway. It was really just a black plastic boom box with a CD player, but it had an equalizer. So that made it a stereo, didn't it?

And unpacking went faster, once that stereo was parked on top of his blue-and-white chest of drawers, filling the room with Guns N' Roses' *Appetite for Destruction*. Eli had bounced around in his pale green tank top and jeans shorts as he arranged his CDs along the top shelves of his two bookcases. The place of pride, just underneath his trophies and the framed picture of him meeting Chris Mullen of the Warriors.

So much space to himself, Eli almost didn't know what to do with it all. Mason had dominated their room in the old house. So Eli had reveled in deciding whether the CDs should be at the near edge of the shelf, ready for action, or parked in the back, like their awesome force was laid back and contained until their disc hit the player.

And when the CDs were away, Eli killed more time figuring out just the right places to put his model X-Wing and TIE Fighter, so they could look like they were dogfighting across the bookshelves.

But now all that was done.

Only the books remained. Mostly finds from library book sales and used book stores, so he could keep more of his money for CDs. (Though, admittedly, Eli bought most of those used too. Allowances only stretched so far.)

Eli knelt on the floor beside his twin pressboard bookshelves, and stared at the small piles of books around him. Science fiction and sports, mostly, which meant he hadn't tapped his vein of fantasy yet.

But then, his few boxes of books were all open, but only half empty while Eli made a half-hearted attempt to figure out how to organize them.

When he'd shared a room with Mason, he only had a little space. So organizing his books had been about cramming as many as he could into as little space as possible. But now he had room to stretch out a bit, and he wasn't sure what approach he liked.

Eli sat back on his heels and twisted his mouth around. He tasted dust, and had to keep wiping sweat out of his eyes and unsticking his tank top. Had to mean it was about noon, right? Time for the grilled cheese sandwiches Mom had promised?

Eli glanced over at his clock. Ten thirty.

Eli sighed. He needed a break. A chance to stretch his legs and do … something else … for a while...

He looked over at the trap door to the attic.

The next thing he knew, Eli was pulling the cord to open the trap door and swing down the rickety stairs.

He kept his sneakers to the outside edge and eased his weight down with each slow step as he ascended, but still the stairs creaked.

He was halfway up when he heard a creak behind him.

Eli whirled so fast his foot slipped off the edge of the stair. Then he was falling toward Byron, who was on the first step.

"Whoa!" yelled Byron, leaping aside as Eli tumbled down to the hardwood floor of the hallway.

Eli landed hard. His left elbow took most of the hit, but his head bonked the floor too. Pain spiked from his funny bone all the way up his arm. Another wave rocked out from his head through his jaw and into his neck.

Byron was laughing, of course, and a moment later Eli realized he could hear Mason laughing too. Meanwhile, Eli lay sprawled on the cherry hardwood, aching and sore. Flexing and stretching his arm through the pain, and going all red faced with shame at the laughter.

Then Dee was suddenly beside him, hands going straight to the elbow. Just her touch made him feel better.

Then he heard something that made him feel worse again.

Mom.

"*What* is going on up here?"

Her words snapped out hard enough that even Mason stopped laughing, and Bryon looked like he was trying to hide behind himself. Eli didn't have the courage to look up at her.

"*Why* is that trap door down?"

"I ... I just..." It sounded too stupid to say though.

"He just wanted a break, Mom," said Dee, rising to his defense. "And none of us have seen the attic yet."

"I have," said Mason. "Nice view."

Mom didn't say anything for a moment, and finally Eli looked up at her. The pain from his arm was abating, but it was going to bruise. And he could tell he was going to have a headache for a while yet.

Mom was standing there, fists on her hips, but the look in her eyes was worried, not angry. She knelt beside Eli, and Dee moved away to give her space.

"Are you all right, baby?" she said, running her fingers over the lump on Eli's head.

Eli nodded.

"All right," said Mom, voice a little softer now. She stood and looked at all four of them, though her eyes darted back and forth between Eli and Dee. "Mason, go get Ava and Roy. Let's all go take a good look at the attic, so you can all see how secure it is."

ONE BY ONE THEY CREAKED UP THE STAIRS. MOM LED THE WAY, MASON next, then Byron. Dee had to come next, so Eli could follow Ava and Roy and make sure they didn't fall like he did.

Dee didn't want to be separated from Eli. Not right now. So much fear from him, before the pain that followed. She wanted to ask if he heard something. Saw something. Byron was still giving him a hard time in a low voice, so maybe it had been nothing. Maybe Eli had just been scared, going up into the attic on his own.

So why didn't he wait for her?

Probably just trying to protect her. He did that sometimes. Took the older-by-a-fraction brother thing a little too seriously. Dee could still remember Sebastian telling her about the warning Eli gave him when she first started dating him.

But then, Dee'd given the same warning to Eli's girlfriends.

But then she was in the attic, and her worries about Eli went to the back burner.

The attic wasn't just big. It was huge! Tall enough in the middle for a maypole, and the back windows were as big as the living room windows had been back in Sunnyvale. There was a stack of boxes along one wall, and even so there was so much space a whole nother family could have lived up here.

Dee kicked herself for not bringing her sketch pad. She'd have to come back up later. In the meantime, she tried to remember attic scenes from some of her favorite romance novels and figure out which of them took place in an attic like this one. Scenes like those would be fun to draw.

"See," said Mom, waving her arms expansively. "Nice and empty."

Mason was at the back windows, clearly looking for something and not finding it. Byron was playing tag with Ava and Roy (Roy was it), all of them smiling and laughing.

Eli was studying the floor around the trap door.

"You won't see any footprints."

"There are a bunch in the dust though."

"No, I mean you won't know which are Dad's or the movers' or even Mason's."

Byron ran past them, hurdling the open trap door.

"That's *enough*," snapped Mom. "We've had all the falls we need for one day. I don't want to find the nearest hospital the hard way. You three want to play tag, do it outside, but be back in for lunch."

"It's too cold up here anyway," said Roy. "Let's go!"

He was right, too. It *was* cold up here. But it was such a warm day...

"If they can play tag," said Mason while the three youngest ran down the stairs, "can I go for a walk?"

"Yes, but be back for lunch. I mean it, Mason. No running off for fast food with the neighbor girl. We have a lot of boxes to get through."

Dee's eyes darted to her oldest brother, who was turning red through the neck and fighting to keep a straight face as he headed for the stairs. *Neighbor girl?* What did he know that they didn't?

Eli didn't even look up at the word of a girl living in their neighborhood. He only had eyes for the floor. But for all his concentration, Dee could tell he wasn't finding anything.

"There was no one up here last night," said Mom, stepping up behind Dee and Eli. "Come look."

She led them to the back windows. They opened, and they were big enough that even a good-sized man could slip through them, but they had screens. And Mom pointed out how to tell that the screens hadn't been taken out for some time.

She also pointed out that it was a sheer drop of some thirty-five or forty feet to the grass below.

Eli looked up at the roof, but shook his head. "That'd take a grappling hook."

Mom laughed, but when neither Dee nor Eli joined her, she said, "Come on, you two. You have to admit that's a pretty funny idea. Someone rappelling down the side of our house so they could go for a walk in the attic?"

Eli snorted. Dee worried at her bottom lip. Mom had a point, but those noises *had* sounded like footsteps.

"Maybe it was nothing," Dee said.

Eli met her eye. She could tell he didn't believe it either. But they had nothing to go on.

A shiver ran through Mom. "It *is* cold up here. Okay, you two. I'm going back downstairs so at least one of us will get a little more done for lunch. Look around to your heart's content, but be down for lunch. Okay?"

"Okay," they said in unison.

"And Eli, I want you to take some aspirin with your lunch. And if you have any headaches or feel even a little bit dizzy, you tell me right away. I mean that. If I think you're holding back, you and I'll go find that hospital this afternoon anyway."

"I swear, Mom." Eli held up the three fingers like a boy scout he'd never been. "I get headaches or dizziness I'll tell you right away."

Mom narrowed her eyes at him, like she thought he might be trying to pull a fast one, but then nodded and went back downstairs.

"What do you think?" Dee said as soon as she heard Mom step off the creaky stairs.

"I don't know." Eli shook his head, then winced. "Doesn't look like anyone could get in and out of here without the trap door."

"You think it was raccoons then? Or pipes?"

Eli shook his head, looking up at the rafters.

"It should be warm up here." Eli looked at her. "Shouldn't it?"

Dee nodded. They both shivered.

"Think maybe we've got a ghost?" he said.

He meant it. She could feel it. But still, Dee couldn't help laughing.

"You've been reading too much sci-fi."

"Well you read too much romance. You and your scenarios."

"At least I don't believe in ghosts." They started back down the trap door stairs. "Come on, you can help me move the big box of books."

"Told you that box was too big."

They were laughing now. And back to the usual disagreements. But still, Dee couldn't shake a chill between her shoulder blades. Here in the light of day it was easy to dismiss the notion of ghosts.

But if Eli had said that last night, Dee knew she would have had a harder time saying no.

LEX WAS ONLY TOO HAPPY TO BE LEAVING THE FACTORY. THEY WEREN'T ready for him. How could they not be ready for him? They were due to start hiring seriously in four weeks — starting work in six — and his office was as bleak as the den in his new home.

They had a desk for him. No *chair* yet, but a desk. And they had a computer, too. Still in boxes. Somewhere. The filing cabinets were set up, but that didn't matter because the files were somewhere else. Probably with the keys to those file cabinets.

Lex had spent the whole morning doing nothing but organizing a move that had nothing to do with settling into his new house. He wondered if Gina would appreciate the irony.

The drive through downtown started to ease some of his frustration and resurrect more of his enthusiasm. This little town of Briar had so much *potential*. Just down Main Street itself he could see three little buildings that just ached for department stores, record stores, book stores, clothing stores.

Why, if the same person bought all three, they could be turned into a small mall. A mall sized just right for Briar. Oh, if only Lex had the money to take advantage of the opportunity himself.

Someday. Someday when he had the C-level job and the income to go with it. Then he'd have the money to become the entrepreneur he was always meant to be.

The town did have a book store already, though, and a diner with a soda fountain, and an honest-to-God five and dime. Lex couldn't remember the last time he'd seen one of those.

And the town even had a little bustle to it. Cars parked up and down Main Street and most of the side streets. People coming and going. His Sable was even the third car in line at the second stoplight through town — the second of two — which for Briar must have constituted a traffic jam.

Cedar Street wasn't nearly as busy for a warm summer day. The only person he saw out for a walk among the lawns and trees was Mason, plainly getting the lay of the land.

Lex lowered his window as he approached.

"Want a lift home?"

Mason just shook his head, and Lex smiled. He should have known better. Why would Mason want to be the geek who takes a ride home from his dad when he can stride around, showing off in shorts and a cut-off tee shirt?

When Lex pulled into his driveway next to the minivan, he noticed the old man across the street. Must have been the one Dee mentioned yesterday. Great big guy with a steely pompadour. He was wearing actual overalls with a red-checked shirt, and sat on his porch in a lawn chair. The kind with an aluminum frame and tiny green and yellow vinyl tubes for cushioning. The porch itself was a faded mustard yellow, same as the rail that edged it. The front door was white though.

The old man made quite a contrast with Lex, in his light gray summer suit, with crisp white shirt and dark blue tie at half-mast.

"Hello there," called Lex as he got out of the car.

"Morning," called the old man back. Gruff voice, but not like he was angry. More like his voice didn't get as much use as most people's.

Lex took the greeting as an invitation and crossed the street. The old man had a small redwood table next to him, with a pitcher of iced tea and a full glass with a sunflower print. Both the glass and the pitcher were sweating the way Lex would if he didn't get out of this suit soon. Had to be pushing ninety out here.

"Lex Dumas," he said, extending his hand. The old man didn't get up, but he leaned forward and shook hands. His grip was strong and his hand rough.

"Name's Barclay," he said, "but most folks just call me Bones, and so can you. Sorry I don't have another chair, but I haven't needed one since Cissy went to be with God."

"That's all right, I don't mind standing." Lex smiled, but uncertain. Should he offer condolences? Bones didn't sound like he needed them. "Been living in the neighborhood long?"

Bones nodded. Lex gave the man a minute, but he didn't seem inclined to go on.

"Have to say, this street is like something out of a storybook. Is it me, or can you smell at least three kinds of flowers?"

"Begonias are the strongest around here, then probably the lavender. If you're getting a third, you're doing pretty good. Much of a gardener?"

"My wife is. And she has plans for the new house, believe you me."

Bones looked like was going to say something, but took a sip of his iced tea instead. Then he shook his head.

"My Cissy's rolling over in her grave at my manners. Can I get you a glass for tea? My house is a might warm, but we could sit in the kitchen while you drink it."

"Thanks, but I should get back. Gina's gonna put *me* in an early grave if I don't help her get the place unpacked. Say, when we do, you should come to dinner. Gina's a wiz in the kitchen. She makes a ziti that will make you think you've gone to Italy."

"That" — Bones swallowed — "that sounds like a right generous offer. Thank you."

Lex blinked at that. The sort of language he used when he was in sales and had to turn something down without sounding like he was turning it down. Or maybe Lex was just being paranoid. Or maybe Bones thought it was an insincere offer and didn't want to show too much enthusiasm.

Either way, he had the feeling that the conversation had run its course.

"I'll get back to you about that dinner in a few days then. Good to meet you."

Bones only nodded at that, but when Lex turned away Bones grabbed his sleeve.

When Lex turned back, the old man had an intense look in his gray eyes. Urgency in his voice.

"I never was a doctor," he said, "but I was a medic through two wars and a police action. You have any problems, *any problems*, I'm right here. Day or night. You understand me?"

"Sure," said Lex, extracting his sleeve. "Thanks."

"I mean it. You and yours show up on my porch at three Ack Emma, I'll invite you right in and do what I can for you."

Weird as this was, the sincerity in the old man's voice touched Lex. When he spoke this time, it was with more warmth.

"Thank you, Bones. And if you need anything, you can let us know too."

Bones nodded, and Lex turned away and started back across the street.

He wasn't sure, but he thought he heard the old man mutter, "Ain't *me* I'm worried about."

***

FINALLY A FEW MINUTES TO HERSELF.

Mason had finally met his neighbor girl — Karina — when he took around the batches of neighbor cookies. And now Mason and Karina were out at a movie — with Eli and Dee in tow. He'd objected, of course, but it was either all of them or none of them as far as Gina was concerned, and Karina's grandparents seemed pleased for the movies to be a group outing rather than a "date" date. This first time anyway.

Truth was, Gina wanted them out of her hair for a little while. She felt bad admitting that, even to herself, but it was true. She could only crack the whip to keep them unpacking for so long before she could feel some of her mother's tones starting to enter her voice.

Always the first warning sign that things were on the verge of going too far. When Gina's own voice reminded her of her mother, it was time to let everyone run around and play a bit.

For Gina, that meant a bath. A long, slow, luxurious bath.

And Lex, God bless the man, understood. He was downstairs right now in the living room with Byron, Ava and Roy, playing Parcheesi.

The master bath was one of Gina's personal selling points on this house. Twin sinks in a swirl of white marble with gold veins. Coral and seashell tiles. A toilet that wasn't in the way of the shower stall, the sinks or the tub.

And a tub that was made of dreams and delight.

Dee had gone on about the tub upstairs, and Gina had to admit that that tub was nice too, but this one was all hers. Wide and long enough for Lex to join her — which had interesting possibilities for the future — it was deep enough to sink into properly without feeling like she might drown. It even had a column of Jacuzzi jets poised to go right down her spine.

Gina had them working on the knots in her back right now, combining with effervescent vanilla and eucalyptus bath salts in a way that felt like heaven. The water had been a little too hot when she got in, but she was used to it now. So good she was getting downright sleepy.

She just lay back with her head in a groove made just for that sort of lounging, and hummed with pleasure.

Lying there she could let go of worries about Dee and Eli, about Eli's bump — just a bump, she was more and more certain — about whatever they'd heard in the attic last night, about how Ava, Roy and Byron would handle the transition to a new town and school, and about how Mason would do off at college in no more than eight short weeks.

She was even able to let go of her worries about whether this new job would be everything Lex said it would. He'd sounded more amused than frustrated with what he'd seen that day at the factory, but she knew him well enough to spot the concerns underneath the humor.

All of that was for later though. Right now was all about this tub of delightful relaxation.

She closed her eyes and began to drift...

Her eyes snapped open. Hands reflexively covering her breasts, even underwater. Shoulders up to protect her neck.

The room was empty.

But she could have sworn...

Just for a moment there, Gina would have sworn that she felt someone in the room with her. Standing over the tub. The door was closed though, and the room was empty. No way anyone could have been standing over her and still disappeared that fast.

She must have been daydreaming. Thinking about those footsteps Eli and Dee said they heard. That was all.

She eased back in the tub again, settling down once more and letting the jets do their work. She inhaled deeply of the vanilla and eucalyptus. Focused on the way the bath salts bubbled along her skin...

Someone loomed over her.

And just like that her eyes were open, but there was nothing to see. Only the tile, and the flickering lights above the counter-length mirror. She strained to hear. Nothing but Lex and the kids in the front room, at their game of Parcheesi. Byron was crowing like he'd just rolled double-sixes.

Gina smiled as she eased back down, and reminded herself to get new light bulbs for this bathroom the next time she or Lex went to the store.

Oh, she shouldn't have thought about the store. Now she was making a list in her head.

And just like that, the tub's spell was broken.

Gina sighed and climbed out, grabbing a fluffy soft white towel from the rack and flipping open the stopper to drain the tub.

She started toweling off while ticking through shopping items in her head. Roy needed new shoes. Byron needed underwear, and so did Ava, who also needed new jeans. That girl wore holes in her jeans faster than any one of her *three* older brothers. And Lex said something about wanting ziti. And the twins needed—

From the corner of her eye, reflected in the mirror, Gina saw a man standing in the shower. Staring at her.

She screamed.

Parcheesi had been a great idea. Gina was always full of great ideas, even when she was actually scheming for richly deserved alone time. It was still a great excuse to play with the kids. So the three of them and Lex sat on the cherry hardwood floor of the living room, between the brown sectional's narrow coffee table and the big, red brick fireplace.

The kids were in their pee-jays. Ava's made her look like an astronaut, while Roy was a cowboy, and Byron even broke out his Spiderman pajamas for the occasion. Lex, of course, was still in jeans, but he had on the tight brown tee shirt that he knew Gina liked. They had a front window open letting in the cool evening air, and they were just about as Norman Rockwell as they ever really got.

Byron was winning, as usual. That kid had more luck with dice than anyone Lex had ever seen. But it didn't matter because they had popcorn and blessedly caffeine-free diet Limon Blast soda, and they were all having a good time.

But then Gina screamed.

And Gina wasn't the type to scream about mice or spiders.

Lex jumped to his feet.

"Byron, you're in charge. You know the rules." Simple enough rules. No answering the door or phone. First sign of trouble get his younger siblings to his room and call the police.

Lex grabbed Mason's maple baseball bat from the umbrella stand by the hall closet and ran barefoot down the hall. He burst through their bedroom door, rolled across their king-size bed, and came to his feet with the bat up and ready to swing.

The bathroom lights were out.

"Gina?" he said, eyes darting everywhere. The bedroom windows were closed. No sign of a prowler.

Then he heard her sobbing. He dropped the bat and went to her. Whatever it was was over.

She was sitting on the bathroom floor, back to the cabinet. Water everywhere around her, chilling his feet. She was still soaking wet. Towel half-wrapped around her. Face buried in her hands.

"Shhh," he said, but when he reached out and touched her shoulder she jumped so hard she banged her head against the cabinet.

"Ow! Lex? Is that you?"

Lex stood and flipped the light switch a couple of times. No lights came on.

"It's me, baby. What happened?"

"I ... I'm not sure."

Lex helped her up and into the bedroom, but she made him fetch a couple of more towels before she was willing to sit on the bed.

And what she told him then didn't make any sense.

"I didn't pass anyone on the way in, and the windows—"

"I know all that, all right? I saw him, and then he wasn't there. And when I turned the lights went out."

"So it was just a trick of the light."

Gina gave him the raised eyebrow. That was a family thing. All the Faranettis that Lex had met could do it. They had a way of arching one eyebrow so it got extra high in the center, a way that identified the person getting the eyebrow as just about the dumbest individual walking this or any other earth.

"All right," he said, hands coming up in surrender. "So it wasn't a trick of the light then. But how can you be—"

"Sure? Well, Lex, honey, if I'm going to imagine a man while I'm naked in our bathroom, he's not going to have skin so white it can't have seen the sun since the turn of the century. And he's not going to have a red, angry scar down the middle of his face, or big sausage hands at the end of even bigger arms—"

"So you've put a lot of thought into the men you imagine while in the bath?"

Levity. The wrong choice here.

"I saw him, Lex. I swear it. I swear it on my grandmother. He was there, standing in our shower. And that's not all..."

But the next thing she told him made even less sense. She could *feel* someone standing over her in the tub? Even though she only needed to open her eyes to...

"That's it," he said. "You got worked up by that odd feeling, and then your imagination ran with it. Gave you the scariest guy you could think of, like a homicidal maniac in your shower. But he wasn't really there, of course, so when you got a proper look he vanished. Just like that feeling."

Gina screwed up her mouth, thinking about that one.

"I want to have a priest come bless the house."

Lex heard all ten of those words, but not one of them made any sense at all.

"What?"

"A priest. You know. A Catholic man, dressed kind of like Johnny Cash but with a white collar. Carries a book you'd never read. Recites prayers in a dead language."

"I know what a..." Lex sighed and tried again. "You want to have a priest come bless the house? Why?"

"Because the kids are hearing footsteps in the attic, and I'm feeling a presence and seeing someone in the mirror who isn't there."

"You're not saying you think this house is haunted."

"It *was* awfully cheap."

Lex flashed on the way Bones didn't want to commit to coming to dinner. Did the old man know something that...

No. That was crazy. There was no such thing as ghosts or hauntings. Lex still remembered all those psychic shows and specials from the 70s, and not one ever proved a damn thing as far as he could tell.

"Gina, that's nuts. You sound like one of your aunts."

"Then maybe it's a Faranetti thing." She shrugged so violently she almost dropped her towel. "Look. I'm not saying I think the house is haunted, and I'm not saying that it isn't. But either way, having a priest bless our new home can't hurt."

Lex blew a breath out through his nostrils. "But I don't want the kids to think—"

"You and the kids never need to see the priest. I'll make the arrangements and you can take the kids into town or something."

She shivered there on the edge of the bed, wrapped in only a wet towel and eyes still wide after her weird experience, whatever happened.

Lex leaned in and kissed her.

"Look, I'm sorry. You say you saw a man, you saw a man. You say you felt a presence, then you did. And if you want a priest to come bless the house, then let's make it happen. I think I passed a Saint Mark's on my way across town. We'll call them first thing in the morning."

Gina wrapped her arms around Lex and clung to him, whispering thank-yous. He was suddenly aware of just how naked she was under that towel, but that was a topic for another time. She'd just been through quite a scare, and he had to go reassure the kids that their mother was all right.

And Lex *would* tell them that, even though he wasn't sure it was true. For crying out loud, she was seeing ghosts and wanting a priest. But there was no way he'd tell his kids that their mother might be cracking up.

She could bring in her priest, and he could say a few words and that should be the end of it.

And if the priest wasn't enough, well, Lex still had Dr. Clyburn's number.

***

DEE TOOK FOREVER TO FALL ASLEEP THAT NIGHT.

She lay there in bed, and stared at the ceiling. Moonlight and the single nearby streetlamp threw dancing shadows across her room as the evening breeze rustled the cedar trees outside the windows on the wall behind her. The closed windows.

She did consider opening one. The breeze would have been nice. The house seemed to hold the evening warmth tonight, even though midnight was closing in rapidly.

But Dee kept her windows shut. She didn't want to listen to the wind in the trees, or the faint rumble and horn of the late night freight train in the distance. Not tonight.

Truth was, she didn't want to listen to *anything*. She wanted to sleep. She wanted the night to pass in an instant while she dreamed of herself as the Pirate Queen, scourge of the seas and despoiler of young noblemen, until the morning sun chased away her fears.

But she had to know.

Dee lay there aware of every little creak of the house and rush of water through pipes. Listening.

Afraid to hear those footsteps again. Just as afraid to not hear them.

She wasn't sure which was worse.

She knew there were no raccoons in the attic. She and Eli had been over every inch. No rats, no raccoons, no ... anything. No droppings or signs of sharp teeth gnawing away or teeny tiny footprints in the dust along the edges of the attic.

Maybe — *maybe* — those were house noises she and Eli heard last night. So if they heard them again, then maybe — *maybe* — it was nothing to worry about. Except that it *could* still have been a stranger in their attic. Wouldn't take more than a ladder and a little effort to get up there. And Dee had never heard any house noises that sounded like footsteps before.

A stranger in the attic could have been looking for something. Something left by a prior owner maybe, or something the stranger stashed up there while the house sat vacant between owners. Maybe under a loose floorboard or something.

Dee and Eli hadn't found any loose floorboards, but that didn't mean anything. They could have missed one.

And if she didn't hear the footsteps again that night? That only meant that someone *had* been up there. There was no other reasonable explanation.

So Dee lay in bed, awake despite her soft flannel sheets and cushy pillows tempting her to sleep. And she listened. Afraid to hear footsteps. Maybe even more afraid not to.

Her heart beat faster, just thinking about it. She glanced across the hall and could see Eli, lying awake just as she was. No doubt thinking the same thoughts. Hoping to avoid a repeat of last night. Especially since they'd been banned from each other's beds, for reasons too disgusting to contemplate.

But lying there and listening wasn't easy. Dee was tired and began to drift. Began thinking back over her evening.

Karina seemed nice enough that Dee could forgive her for being drop-dead gorgeous, but it would have been nice to not have Mason there to dominate the conversation. In all fairness, though, Karina seemed as into Mason as he was into her.

Even in the middle of nowhere, the beautiful people can find each other. Only the plainer Janes like Dee would have to struggle to find guys worth dating. Typical.

And though Karina did have a brother, he was back home in Sacramento and not down here at their grandparents' place for the summer like she was. He had some kind of science camp thing, and couldn't get away.

At least the movie hadn't been scary. *Indiana Jones and the Last Crusade*. Good triumphing over evil and all that kind of stuff. Could have used a better romance plot though. Sean Connery and Harrison Ford both with the same girl who was decades younger than either of them? Yeah, they were manly and all, but come on.

Sparse crowd at the theater, so Dee hadn't even gotten a good look at the locals. And whatever they put on their popcorn was definitely not butter. Ick.

Then after the movie, Mason and Eli spent the whole drive home arguing about whether or not the ending meant that Indy and his father were now immortal. Would have been a total waste there except for a shared moment with Karina. A shared look of exasperation that could have been summed up in one word: *boys*.

That was cool though. Maybe Karina could make a good friend, if Mason didn't blow it while dating her...

creak

Was that a footstep?

Eli was sitting up in his bed across the hall. Dee sat up, and even across distance and shadows she could feel eye contact with him. They were like one person in that moment. One set of lungs breathing fast and shallow. One heart rushing blood through one set of veins. One set of ears straining for the next—

creak ... creak

Definitely footsteps. Slow, but heavy. Moving away from the trap door.

Moving her direction.

Dee was out of bed and across the hall before her covers hit the floor. Then she and Eli were clinging to each other, her atop the covers and him under them.

Neither of them said a word. Dee wasn't sure either of them even breathed. They huddled together, hearts racing.

More footsteps. Closer now.

In the hallway.

A shadow filled the doorway.

The overhead light flipped on, and Dee squeezed her eyes shut against the sudden glare.

"Eli do you hear..." Mason's voice, harsh with whisper. "What the hell?"

Dee forced her eyes open. There stood Mason in the doorway wearing only a pair of blue nylon sweats. He held an aluminum baseball bat in one hand.

Mason stepped into the room and closed the door behind him.

"So you heard that too?" said Eli in a quiet voice. "The footsteps in the attic?"

Mason nodded. "I'm going to go check it out. You wanna come with?"

"Mom said to get Dad," said Dee before Eli could say something stupid, showing off for their big brother.

"Fine. I'll stand guard under the trap door then. Eli, you get Dad. Dee," — Mason pointed the bat at her — "you better get back to your own bed. Mom's not going to let that go."

Dee started to say something, but changed her mind. She hadn't realized Mason could hear Mom's lecture that morning, but she wasn't surprised. Nothing seemed to get past him. But at least he seemed to understand.

Mason opened the door and stood by where the trap door steps would open, bat up and ready like he's expecting a pitch. Eli zipped down the hall for the back stairs. And Dee went back to her own bed to shiver.

When had it gotten cold? Wasn't it warm just a little while ago?

Dad wasn't thrilled about getting rousted, but he came up in his tartan bathrobe with Mason's maple bat in one hand and a flashlight in the other. Mom came up too, checking on the little ones like she thought there might really be an intruder, despite all her laughter that morning.

In fact, Mom didn't look like this was a laughing matter at all. She had that wrinkled brow look, like when Mason was out past curfew and she was pacing in the living room. She was whispering when she checked on Dee, and even asked what Dee saw.

Dee was too scared to answer. Just shook her head and tapped her ear to say she'd heard, not seen.

Mom nodded over at Dad then, and Dad pulled down the cord to open the trap door.

Dee practically bit through her lip when Dad scaled the stairs. Her heart was pounding like she'd just finished a floor routine and was waiting for the scores from unhappy looking judges.

Well, if what she was hearing now was footsteps in the attic — Dad and Mason coming off of the stairs — then she'd definitely heard footsteps earlier.

"Nothing," Dad called down. Moments later he creaked back down the stairs, Mason in tow. "There's no one up there guys, and it doesn't look like anyone *has* been."

Dad closed the trap door, put an arm around Mom, and called the three eldest children over to him. He spoke in hushed words.

"I don't know what you three heard, but it couldn't have been footsteps."

"It sounded just like you and Mason walking around up there," said Eli, "only it was one person, not two."

Dee nodded.

"Regardless," said Dad. "The attic is secure, and we all need our sleep. So you guys turn in." He looked at Mom, then continued. "Tomorrow I'm going to take the bunch of you over to Monterey and the aquarium. We'll have a good old time and get the scare out of your systems, and your mom will stay here while we have a contractor check it out and see if he can do something about the creaking. All right?"

"You're *sure* that's all it is?"

"What else could it be?" said Mom, but she didn't sound confident like she had that morning.

Eli opened his mouth to say something, then.shook his head.

"Exactly," said Dad. "Honest, guys, it's just a new house with some new sounds. By next week they'll be gone or they'll be old hat and you won't even think about them anymore."

Dee doubted that, but there was nothing more to say. She went back to her own bed, while Eli and Mason returned to theirs and Mom and Dad went back downstairs.

Dee did her best to calm down enough to sleep, but just when she was almost ready to zonk out, she heard it.

One more footfall in the attic. Over by the little windows in the front of the house.

Dee looked over at Eli, who looked right back at her.

Neither one of them fell asleep for some time.

3

Tuesday June 13th, 1989. Day Two.

Lex stared at his tartan-robed reflection in the bathroom mirror while he brushed his teeth that morning. Six round light bulbs above the big mirror over the twin sinks, putting out way more light than they needed to. Even with the bathroom's sole window on the west side of the house, the sunlight was ample for his morning routine.

But Lex had wanted to see if the lights flickered.

They were nice and steady.

He had to admit that was odd. Gina said they flickered on her, and he himself had flipped that light switch four or five times when he found her on the floor in the dark last night. No response then, even though the breakers were fine when he checked on them later.

Had to be a loose wire or something. One bank of lights going dark for a while was no evidence of a haunted house. Of all things.

Lex kept glancing toward the shower stall as he brushed the minty foam around in his mouth. Trying to get that corner-of-the-eye effect. Yeah, there were shadows in the shower, but nothing that could look like a man. Much less a shockingly pale man with an angry red scar down his face. He sure hadn't seen or felt anything odd during his shower.

But then, Lex hadn't fallen asleep in the bathtub and had a bad dream.

Poor Gina. She was so shaken up she hardly slept. And she was already dressed and gone while Lex was getting in his morning exercise: push-ups, sit-ups and lunges. Still, if letting her bring in a priest to scatter some holy water and say a few words gave her peace of mind, then she could bring one in every day for a month.

Just so long as the kids didn't see it happen. Lex knew that Gina's family was Catholic, but he'd never had any use for his parents' Presbyterian ways, and didn't see why the Catholics were any better.

God was a fiction Alexander Dumas did not need. And he would not push it on his kids. Much less the level of superstition that led to house blessings to drive away evil spirits.

Lex let all of that go as he threw on a Giants shirt, cargo shorts with lots of pockets, and a good pair of Birkenstocks. Perfect attire for a day by the ocean while Gina let her shaman play ghost-be-gone.

Mason already had the kids organized when Lex reached the kitchen. Everyone had a bowl of cereal and a glass of orange juice. They were even sitting in something like an order around the dining room table, though Byron, Ava and Roy were all bouncing in their chairs, super-excited at the prospect of seeing otters.

Ava and Roy had made a chant out of it. "Otters, otters, *otters*," like it was a conga line. Better here than in the car. The drive would be long enough as it was.

Oh, who was he kidding? They'd be chanting in the car too, and Byron would probably join them.

Heck, even Lex might join them. Better than fighting it when he wanted to lift everyone's spirits.

Lex was looking forward to the bat ray petting pool, himself. He found something very appealing about getting to stroke a wild sea creature like a pet.

"Thanks, Mason," he said, clapping his eldest on the shoulder and getting a bowl for himself. Mason had an A's tee shirt on, which was no surprise. They were having as good a year as the Giants, maybe. More surprising was that Mason hadn't gotten around to cropping this shirt yet. It fell all the way to his waist. He had on his jean shorts though. In fact, all the kids had their shorts on, and light tee shirts too.

He'd have to remember to make them bring windbreakers. The day was warming up here in Briar, but the sea air could get awfully breezy.

Lex got a good look at his three eldest as he sat down to join the whole crew at the table. Mason looked tired, like he'd been up too late studying or something, but Eli and Dee looked downright haggard and seemed constantly fighting to not yawn. He almost wanted to send them back to bed, but that wasn't an option, given that a priest might come wandering through, blessing up the place.

"We get back," said Lex, pointing with his spoon, "and you two are taking naps. You're not sleeping enough."

The twins shared a look, then shrugged and nodded. It was as though those two could hold whole conversations together without ever having to say a word. Now *that* was a truly weird thing. Odd noises in the attic, things seen out of the corners of the eye, those things could be explained away by the new house.

But the way Dee and Eli seemed to almost read each other's minds? That was something else. Lex had known three sets of twins in the course of his life. Two sets in high school — including the Angulo sisters, and he'd dated Linda Angulo — and one in college. None of them, *none of them*, had ever been as close as Dee and Eli.

Lex might have to push for them to go to separate colleges. They needed time apart, or they'd never find husbands and wives of their own. They'd end up unmarried, living together and suffering the rumors that would come with that.

Lex shook his head. He was worried about nothing. They were clinging together because they were scared, but once everything was back to normal school would start. Then they'd make new friends, find dates, join their sports teams ... do the little independent things that separated them instead of sticking only to the things that brought them together.

And if they stayed close though fulfilling lives, wasn't that a good thing? Lex wouldn't mind being closer to his own brother, however often their diverging political views drove them apart.

"Why isn't Mom coming?" said Ava. "She loves otters too."

"I told you," said Mason, "she has to meet the contractor."

"When you need work done," said Lex, "the contractors get the power to say when it happens."

Byron looked like he had a follow-up question, but Lex started urging them to finish breakfast and start the toilet brigade so they could hit the road. Then they were all shoveling down cereal like there were prizes at the bottom of the bowls.

They'd be on the road in no time. The trip would give Gina all the time she needed. Assuming priests did same-day service...

———

GINA HAD BEEN TO MANY CHURCHES AND CATHEDRALS WHEN SHE WAS growing up. She knew the look, knew what to expect. High peaked roofs, ornate stonework. Statuary, arches, gargoyles. Huge stained glass windows. A bell tower.

The sweeping majesty of God expressed through architecture.

Which was why when Gina pulled the Sable into the Saint Mark's parking lot, she was sure she had the wrong place. Yes, the sign out front read "Saint Mark's" but, well, it looked less like a masterwork of architecture and more like the place architects did their work.

Or maybe a warehouse. It might have been a warehouse.

Either way, it was a gray, square building, maybe three stories tall and without so much as an arch or a tower. It might have had a stained glass window or two, but Gina couldn't get a good look at the row of windows high up.

It did have a bible quote on the side that faced the parking lot. John 3:16, she knew it well. She'd memorized it in Catechism class. She could have recited it even without the letters painted in gold scrollwork.

"For God so loved the world that He gave His only begotten Son that whosoever believeth in Him shall not perish, but shall have everlasting Life."

That wasn't a proper Catholic thing either. Protestant churches waved Bible verses around that way, not good Catholic cathedrals.

Gina pulled into a parking spot and grabbed her big black leather purse from the passenger seat. She had to dig around for a moment to find her notepad, but not as long as Lex would have made the search sound.

She flipped the notebook open to the right page. Checked the address. Checked it again.

This had to be the right place, though Gina had to admit that it wasn't exactly filling her with confidence, much less the Holy Spirit.

It definitely wasn't across the street. That was a row of little businesses. A donut shop, a barber (*not* a hair salon, as the sign emphasized), two dry cleaners and a Theo's Greek Deli.

Only two other cars in the parking lot with her, both of them compact cars. A Toyota and a Honda. Could a priest drive a foreign car? Maybe if it was Italian...

Gina shook her head, checked her makeup, and got out of the car. She'd dressed to meet a priest. Long black skirt down to her ankles, conservative navy blue blouse, and black flats. Not even a drop of perfume, just her scentless "ladies" deodorant.

She should have put on something. Even a little. As it was, she smelled like her closet.

The sky was clear and blue, and the breeze felt like it was gearing up for a warm day. The blacktop parking lot was clean as she crossed it, idly wondering how this little town managed enough trade to support two dry cleaners. A nothing question to distract herself from more urgent concerns.

Concerns that came rushing back as she stood outside the double front doors. They should have been carved wood. Instead they were plain and a dull red, with tarnished brass handles.

Gina honestly wondered if she should knock. She'd never knocked on a church door before, but this place was so strange she wasn't sure.

She shook her head, mustered her courage, and opened the door.

At first glance, the inside was as disappointing as the outside.

Thin, carpeted floors? No stonework at all?

Just the kind of beige carpeting that put her in mind once more of office buildings.

Gina wanted to sigh, but held it in. Still, her mother would have thrown a fit if she saw this narthex. It was wide enough, sure, and with such width it had just enough depth that fifty or sixty parishioners could have milled about before or after services.

But the ceiling was low, maybe eight feet up. And the walls and ceilings were a muddy brown color. Cork board on the wall to her left, covered in fliers for Sunday school plays and an upcoming potluck.

And bingo. Maybe this was a Catholic place after all.

Under the cork board was a table draped in white cloth, with an offering box, a display case with crucifixes, rosaries and saint statues, and a half-empty sign-up sheet for something.

Hall leading off each direction. Three double-doors spaced apart in front of her, no doubt leading to aisles down the nave.

Those doors were nice, stained wood, with carved handles and those little metal things up top that would make sure they closed quietly during a service. Maybe there was hope for this place yet.

Which was good, because, honestly, if the sign hadn't identified the building as the right place — and if the yellow pages hadn't insisted it was a Catholic church — Gina would have already run off to look for someplace else.

As it was, she was still considering doing just that. Gilroy wasn't all that far, and it had to have a proper cathedral. And if it didn't, maybe she'd look as far afield as Monterey. Monterey was part of the mission trail. They *had* to have a proper—

The double doors in front of her opened.

Stepping through came a young priest, not more than a few years older than Mason. He had a tanned but pockmarked face, short black hair, and big brown eyes that looked too big on his skinny frame. He was carrying manila folders so overstuffed with papers he needed both hands to corral them.

But he smiled when he saw her, and that smile did more to relax Gina than any of the words that followed it. That first smile held everything that Gina remembered from the best priests during her childhood — serenity and humor, patience and understanding.

"Be welcome here," he said. "I'm Father Andrew. How may I help you?"

Everything tried to rush out of Gina at the same time. All of it. From the terrifying experience in the bathroom to the "footsteps" in the attic to worries about each of her children and her husband and the new town and the new job and the new house which might have been haunted even though she didn't believe in ghosts or didn't want to believe anyway but the evidence was starting to mount up in her head and...

So very many things tried to come out of Gina's mouth at the same time that they blocked each other. She opened her mouth, and all that came out was a sob. Then she was crying, and feeling like an idiot because she shouldn't have been crying in front of a stranger even if he was a priest. But it was all just *too much*.

Then the priest was holding her. Not in any weird way, just his arms around her, hands on her shoulders, and letting her cry. He made soothing little sounds while she bawled, until finally, after what felt to Gina like five or six hours, her tears finally ran dry.

The priest let go of her then and said in a soft tone, "Would you prefer the confessional or my office?"

"Your papers," Gina said, realizing Father Andrew had dropped his folders, and the papers were scattered everywhere across the carpet.

"Don't worry about that. The papers will wait."

"Your office. I guess."

Gina followed Father Andrew through the nave and back behind the altar to his office. Along the way she was pleased to note that two of the windows were stained glass. One an image of Christ in the garden at Gethsemane and the other of Saint Mark on the road to

Alexandria. The pews were solid maple, the ceiling was good and high, and the altar had a proper crucifix.

So at least the worship area looked right. Even if it had only a single confessional, off to the right.

Father Andrew's office was small, with barely enough room for a narrow desk with a phone, two folding visitors' chairs, and a pressboard bookcase full of religious texts, not all of which were Christian. Some, like the *Nag Hammadi Library* she didn't recognize at all.

Father Andrew noticed her looking over the titles.

"People find God many ways. The more I understand their paths, the more I understand the people." He smiled at her again. "How can I help you?"

Gina's heart started pounding. This was all so ridiculous? How could she sit here with a priest and tell him her house was haunted? She could feel herself flush, and licked her lips nervously.

"This ... this doesn't look like any Saint Mark's I've ever seen."

"I don't doubt it," he said with a chuckle. "Briar had a fine old cathedral, but it burnt down last year. No one was hurt, by the grace of God, but that was how we ended up here." He looked up as though he could see the whole of the building from where he sat. "With time and help from the faithful, we'll make this place our own. But in the meantime, it serves."

"My house is haunted."

Father Andrew didn't chuckle now. He just looked at her, patience in those brown eyes, and listened while Gina poured out the whole story. The footsteps, the presence, the scary pale scarred apparition. All of it. Even her concerns about Eli and Dee sharing a bed.

When she finished, Gina wasn't even looking at the priest. She couldn't. She just stared down at her black flats, her shoulders sagging as though she'd just dropped a two-hundred-pound load.

So Gina did not see the look on Father Andrew's face when he picked up his phone and buzzed someone.

"Angela?" he said. "Would you reschedule the glaziers and the carnival committee meeting for me? There's something I need to look into."

Something was up. Eli was sure of it.

First, Dee got shotgun instead of Mason for the drive to Monterey. That was an interruption of the natural order. When Mom wasn't riding shotgun, the seat went to Mason as the oldest. Then Eli and Dee in the middle row, and Byron stuck in the back with Ava and Roy.

Dee only ever got shotgun if Mom and Dad wanted to separate her and Eli. They never admitted that, of course. There was always some excuse about her being the eldest girl or something.

But it was true anyway.

Eli had already been suspicious of this whole trip. Everyone but Mom going to Monterey? Mom stuck back at the house to meet with a "contractor?"

Yeah, it was a believable enough story. Mom was usually the one who met with contractors. Hell, she was related to most of them, and spoke their language with the fluency of a native.

But nobody said anything about a contractor at dinner last night. And none of the usual signs were there, like Mom complaining about a toilet, or the lights, or...

Well, it *was* a new house. Maybe they already had the appointment to get something fixed, and just didn't think about it last night. Just saw it on the calendar this morning.

But it still sounded fishy.

Didn't help that Dad was acting too happy on the drive to Monterey. Eli could always tell, and he needed only quick eye contact with Dee in the rear view mirror to know that she saw the same signs he did.

Singing along with that "otters" chant Ava and Roy started? Going on about the bat petting pool? Even talking about getting salt water taffy for everyone when they were barely on the freeway?

Something was up, all right.

Eli leaned closer to Mason, who had his nose buried in a Clive Barker novel. Eli nudged Mason until he looked up, then whispered.

"What do you think Mom's really doing?"

"Meeting with a contractor. Mom's already unhappy with the kitchen cabinets."

"Mmmmaybe."

Mason stuck his finger in his book and turned to face Eli. "What do you think then?"

Eli shrugged.

"Check out the barn, kids!" said Dad making everyone look out the window to the left.

It was a barn all right. Big, with a peaked roof and faded red paint. White exes painted on double doors large enough to admit a tractor.

"Horses or cows?" Dad said.

The standard long drive game. Pick a building and guess what it holds, then support the guess. Too easy in this case. The fields around the barn made it pretty obvious.

"Hay," said Mason, at the same time Dee and Eli said it. Ava guessed horses, and Roy and Byron were too busy thumb wrestling to answer.

"Why horses?" Dad asked Ava, who ignored the question and launched into a long description of the kinds of beautiful horses she imagined lived happily together in the barn, including one winged horse, their leader, who went out flying every day at dusk to make sure that none of the sheep got lost.

That last was the only part, in Eli's opinion, that even touched on reality. They could all see the field full of sheep next to the hay fields, although Eli suspected that the sheep belonged to the next farm over.

Either way, he waited until Dad got a sing-a-long of *Africa* by Toto going before whispering to Mason again.

"I think it's got something to do with the attic. She's meeting with the cops maybe."

"There was no one up there, Eli. We had a good look."

"What were those footsteps then?"

"Come on, you two," cut in Dad. "Our harmonies need some help in the mid-range."

No choice then. Eli and Mason had to join in the sing-a-long, and

Dad kept the songs going until he found a parking spot along Cannery Row in Monterey.

Then, with the aquarium right in front of him, even Eli couldn't help getting caught up in the excitement. Sharks and eels and yes, otters.

He and Mason went straight for the shark tank the moment Dad got them inside, while Dee led Ava and Roy to the otters and Dad took Byron to see the dolphins.

With so much to do and see and talk about, not to mention lunch along Cannery Row and Dad making good on his promise of salt water taffy, it was hours before Eli even gave another thought to the house and whatever Mom might be doing back there.

FATHER ANDREW BROUGHT A BROWN BRIEFCASE WITH HIM, THOUGH HE left it in the kitchen, on the counter, while Gina showed him the house.

Father Andrew said nothing while Gina showed him the bathroom where she saw the apparition, and how the lights seemed to be fine now no matter how they behaved last night. He did try the switch himself, and seemed satisfied that the lights were working now.

He didn't even comment on the too-much lavender potpourri Gina had arranged in two dishes — one on the lip of the extra-large bathtub and one on the white marble counter between the two sinks — to try to soothe her when she found it necessary to come in.

Father Andrew said nothing as she led him up the stairs, and only nodded and paid close attention as she showed him the attic. He listened attentively, but without any clear reactions, as Gina talked about the footsteps Eli, Dee and Mason had heard.

It wasn't until the two of them were back in the kitchen, leaning against the cherry-wood counters and sipping instant coffee — saccharine in Gina's, black for the priest — that he even asked a question.

"Did you notice any odd smells when you felt the presence or saw ... what you saw?"

Gina shivered, just remembering, but shook her head.

"All right." He inhaled deeply, let the breath out slowly. "I know you felt a presence, and I don't doubt it was frightening. But I have to ask, did you notice any other feeling? Anything at all?"

Gina had to think about that one. "Nothing then, but..."

"Yes?"

Gina shook her head. "It's nothing, I'm sure."

"Please. Tell me."

He had such patience in those eyes, that Gina twisted her mouth, embarrassed, but answered.

"Last night, when Lex and I went up to see about those footsteps. Well. It was cold."

"But last night was a warm night."

"I know. It's stupid. I—"

"You may finish that thought if you wish, but I believe you misunderstand me."

Gina blinked at the priest.

"You did not say you felt a chill. You did not say you shivered. You said it was cold. But the evening was warm. Were you alone in feeling this cold?"

"No," Gina said slowly. "I saw Lex tie his robe tighter. Why?"

Father Andrew set his cup down on the counter, and Gina couldn't help a fleeting wish to paint the cupboards just for a break in the all-wood décor.

Father Andrew tapped his chin, brow furrowed, then spoke.

"Those who believe in spirit activity often say that the presence of spirits is accompanied by lowered temperatures. 'Cold spots' they call them, when they persist, but sometimes a room is said to chill when a spirit is active."

"So you think my house *is* haunted?"

"That's not for me to say," he said with a shake of his head. "But I will bless this house, every room if you like. And in case there *are* any restless spirits, I will perform the last rights, which should lay them to rest."

Effusive thanks bubbled out of Gina, but Father Andrew waved them away.

"I should tell you. I have heard some talk of this house before. Past owners have not stayed here long, and their neighbors don't speak about those owners as 'moving' but as 'fleeing.'"

"So the house *is* haunted."

"Again, that's not for me to say. I only felt obligated to tell you that it has a history, of sorts. Though I don't know if knowing that history will help you. So far as I know, your predecessors did not seek the aid or blessings of the Church. You have. So let us see what can be done."

Father Andrew faced the counter and opened his brief case. Inside he had a silver aspergillum with a dark wooden handle, holy water, a bible, a prayer book, a small bottle of communion wine, and a container of communion wafers.

He turned back around, and for the first time Gina saw the priest's brow furrow.

"It would be better if you were shriven before we begin. As you certain you won't give confession?"

"I think Lex would have a fit."

"Yet he *does* know I'm here? He'll agree to let a priest bless his house?"

"He agreed to let *me* have a priest bless *our* house. Believe me, the less involvement Lex has with the whole process, the happier we'll all be."

Father Andrew tapped his chin and frowned.

"Was he baptized?"

"Yes. Presbyterian. I don't think he meant it when he took confirmation though, and he really doesn't believe these days. But ... that doesn't matter, does it?"

"And your children?"

"Only Mason's been baptized. My eldest. After him, Lex wouldn't..."

The priest's eyes widened as though Gina had just confessed to being a witch.

"What's the matter?" said Gina.

"Your children should be baptized. As soon as possible. You said they're in Monterey? If they were to be hit by a truck on the drive home..."

"Lex will never allow it." Gina sighed. "He wants them to make up their own minds. He won't have me 'pushing my family's beliefs' on them." Then a cold knot settled in her gut. "But ... you'll still bless the house..."

"It's not for me to tell you how to raise your children," said Father Andrew, raising his hands. "And of course I will still bless your house. I would never turn away a soul in trouble. But I would remind you that faith is a shield against the worries that assail us, especially those of a spiritual nature. Unbaptized children, a husband without faith in the Almighty, these are like holes in your shield. I may cleanse your house, but only you can keep it clean."

Gina shivered at that thought, but Father Andrew wasn't quite finished.

"And I would like you to think about something. When you found yourself with trouble — something beyond what you think of as the everyday world — you turned to the Church for help. And the Church is here for you. But what about your children? Without the Church, where will they turn for help?"

Gina blinked, struck by the fear she'd seen in Eli's eyes when he came to get Lex last night. The fear that drove Dee into his bed the night before.

Gina thought about that as the priest began to move through the house, offering prayers in Latin and sprinkling holy water.

She thought about it a lot.

"You've got to be kidding me."

And here Lex thought the night was going well.

After a good day in Monterey — complete with a fish and chips lunch for everyone along the docks — Lex had come home to a much calmer Gina.

Or at least she'd seemed that way at the time. Smiling and laughing, and spinning some quick story about a contractor who'd tightened some loose boards in the attic walls that were shifting with the wind and creaking like footsteps.

Lasagna for dinner, and a night off from unpacking for everyone. The kids went out exploring the neighborhood together, and Gina practically jumped Lex the minute they were alone.

If that sudden outpouring of passion was the result of having a priest over, she could invite this "Father Andrew" over every day.

And the priest must have settled Gina's mind about the bathroom. She actually took a bath after they finished and the youngest kids got home, while Lex entertained Byron, Ava and Roy with what had to be their ten thousandth viewing of *Star Wars* on video. But Gina had her nice long soak, without any screaming or panicking at all.

The older kids got back when they were supposed to, and everybody turned in more or less on time.

This was the kind of day Lex was hoping for when they came down here. Good family fun. And a chance to see the neighborhood gave the kids something normal to talk about. Even Eli and Dee seemed more relaxed tonight, though Eli still poked around with an echo of the suspicion Lex had seen in him on the drive that morning.

Finally the evening was done, and Gina and Lex reclined together in their fluffy, king-size bed, the only lights coming from their twin reading lamps, one at each end of the mahogany headboard. The covers were down, and the sea foam green cotton sheets still rumpled from their romp. The heavy green curtains were still closed as well, and despite the warmth of the evening Lex felt no need to open them.

In between the bed and the windows, they each still had a stack of boxes in their respective corners, only half their clothes unpacked and none of their books or personal knickknacks. There'd been too much to do in the rest of the house. Fortunately, the bedroom was more than large enough to accommodate the boxes alongside their nice mahogany bureaus and Gina's antique redwood armoire.

But the unpacking could wait.

Gina had on her flimsy pink nightie as though she might have been considering round two. She smelled like that coconut and aloe lotion she liked so much, and Lex had to admit he'd developed some very good associations with those scents. Almost to the point that he had to be careful when they went to the beach or risk an embarrassing development in his trunks.

Lex only had on his striped boxers — the way she liked him to sleep — and was just about to see if that nightie were, in fact, a hint, when she dropped the bomb on him.

Now they were both sitting up. And from the look in her eye, she wasn't kidding him.

"No," she said, undaunted by the disbelief in Lex's voice. "I'm serious. I think we should baptize the kids."

"One meeting with a priest, and you're ready to go whole hog back to the Catholics? Wish *my* sales force was that good."

"Don't joke about this. I understand you don't believe—"

"I haven't heard you crying to get up early on Sundays and haul ass down to church."

Gina folded her arms. "May I finish?"

This was not good.

Lex gave a slow nod.

"I understand that you don't believe. But how can our children decide what they believe if we don't expose them to any beliefs at all?"

"I think your parents more than make up for it when they visit. Your mother can't drink a glass of water without praying over it first."

"That's because her Aunt Ida..." Gina shook her head. "That's beside the point. The whole point of baptism is to protect the children's souls until they're old enough to make up their own minds and either affirm the promises made on their behalf, or walk away."

"You see one shadow in the mirror and suddenly you're worried about souls?"

"I knew you'd mock this."

"How can I not?" Lex threw up his hands. "Listen to yourself, babe. This priest has you thinking in circles. You wanted the house blessed? Fine, it's been blessed. But like a salesman, the priest isn't happy with the low-end deal. He wants to sell you all the upgrades."

Lex blew out a breath.

"It's just a con, baby. It's all just a con they run on people who are scared."

"Like me."

"Normally I'd say no. Normally I'd say my Gina is a strong, independent woman who doesn't need to believe in some invisible friend to get her through the day. But ... something spooked you last night."

Uh oh, now he was getting the raised eyebrow. He could feel sweat already collecting at the back of his neck and an itch between his shoulder blades.

Tread carefully, Lex.

"And I get it. I completely get it. The kids were already nervous, and you saw something — you definitely saw something and I'm not saying you didn't—"

"So what *are* you saying?"

Oh, that was a frosty tone. Frosty enough to damn near gel the sweat on his back.

But that sweat kept coming.

"I'm saying every strong person has a weak moment here and there. And this Father Andrew pounced on your moment like a cat on a mouse. Now he's in your head and has you thinking all kinds of crazy thoughts."

Not a single crack in her stoic expression.

"Well, I'm not sure I want to share my bed with a man who thinks I'm weak."

"I don't think you're weak. Hell, you're stronger than I am. It's just—"

Gina picked up Lex's pillow and shoved it against his chest.

"But—" he tried, but she cut him off again.

"We'll try this conversation again in the morning. Assuming you're willing to have a civilized discussion."

"But—"

"Couch." And Gina pointed to the bedroom door.

Lex sagged from the shoulders up. He sighed. But he grabbed his tartan bathrobe from the closet before he began the long trudge down the hall to the living room.

At least he wouldn't need a blanket. Not warm as this evening was.

AS MIDNIGHT APPROACHED, DEE LAY IN BED, HER MIND WANDERING.

She knew she should stay awake. Knew she should listen for the footsteps again. Should be ready to call Dad and Mason, just in case. After all, maybe they hadn't found anyone in the attic last night, but the footsteps stopped when they went up, and she heard only one more after they came back down.

Whatever was going on up there, investigating seemed to make it stop.

Unless investigation was what it wanted?

Dee rolled on her side and punched her soft pillow. She threw off her thin summer blanket. Even that was too much for the evening warmth.

Honestly. Worrying about what footsteps wanted?

That was just crazy talk. No reason to start ascribing motivations when she didn't even know what was going on. And Mom claimed the noise was just loose boards in the attic, shifting in the wind and creaking. Mom said the noise only *sounded* like footsteps. Said her contractor took care of the issue.

So if Mom was right, Dee could lie here awake all night and never hear a footstep.

Dee glanced across the hall. Eli wasn't looking back.

Was he asleep? That would be a good sign. If Eli was comfortable enough to fall asleep, then maybe it was safe for Dee to sleep too.

Anyway, staying up all night was a bit much to consider, tired as she was from little sleep the last two nights and such a big day today. Monterey and the aquarium. Lunch and shopping on Cannery Row.

Walking all over the place with Eli, Karina, and Mason. Even playing on the swings in that park a block-and-a-half over.

Still, maybe Dee should hang on for midnight. Just in case. If midnight came and went without her hearing any more footsteps, then maybe Mom was right. Maybe it was just a few loose boards...

Except the wind blew in the daytime too, and Dee only heard the footsteps at night.

A small thought, but the kind of detail that should have dug in and held on. That little fact should have been enough to make Dee shiver, make her heart rate pick up. That was certainly how the last couple nights had gone.

Should have been enough to keep her awake. Maybe even enough to wake up Eli.

But she kept drifting. The fact was, Dee felt more comfortable lying there in bed that night than she'd felt since they got to Briar.

And Karina played soccer. Dee smiled. They'd had a whole conversation Mason couldn't interrupt. Probably couldn't even follow. Though he hung on Karina's every word anyway, instead of going off with Eli to check out the chain-link nets on the park's basketball court and examine the blacktop surface. But then, Eli wasn't trying to score with Karina.

He might have, though. If she hadn't already been making eyes at Mason. Just as well. Eli never won when he competed for girls with Mason. Besides, if Eli didn't date Karina, Dee might have a better friendship with her.

It was true that the best girlfriends for Eli were the ones who could be good friends with Dee, but it was also true those friendships ended the moment the relationships did.

Staying friends with Eli's exes was no more possible for Dee than it was possible for Eli to stay friends with one of Dee's exes. Sebastian was the perfect example. He used to play pick-up basketball with Eli every Saturday morning. But the moment Dee started souring on the relationship, suddenly Eli found other commitments on Saturday mornings. And she'd never had to say a word...

What was that noise?

Dee lay still. She listened as hard as she could.

She could hear the wind in the cedar trees outside. She could hear the faint horn of a distant freight train. She could hear the rumble of a motorcycle out on the freeway. She could hear her own heart beating faster now, and her breaths going in and out her nose.

Maybe it was nothing?

Dee looked across the hall again. This time Eli was looking back.

She couldn't see his eyes, not in the dim evening light, but she didn't need to. She could feel eye contact with Eli. Could tell he was awake, mirroring the way she was curled around her pillow, her on her left side and Eli on his right. His blanket was down too. They were both only under their sheets.

Eli was awake. But did he hear ... whatever she heard? Or was he responding to her nerves?

Eli shook his head. Slow. Deliberate.

He was responding to her then. He hadn't heard anything. Dee shrugged.

Eli kept the connection. Kept the eye contact. That eased some of the tension out of Dee's shoulders. Together they lay there, looking at each other across the hall. Waiting.

And the noise came again.

It wasn't a footstep. And it wasn't coming from the attic. In fact, it was so normal sounding Dee almost wondered why she noticed it at all.

It was a scratching sound. Coming from outside. Not along the two windows behind her bed, but the walls.

Scratch scratch ... Scratch scratch

To the right of the windows, toward her closet. It might almost have been coming from her chest of drawers, but she could tell that wasn't it. It was coming from outside the house. Along the wall there.

Dee shivered. Reached for her blanket.

"What do you think?" Eli's voice, a harsh whisper from her doorway. He stood there, silhouetted in only his purple pajama bottoms.

"Raccoons?" Dee shrugged and sat up, blanket pulled up to her neck.

There was a break in the scratching, and Eli walked over and sat on the edge of the bed next to Dee.

"Whatever it is, I don't think it can get in."

Dee shook her head.

"I could open the window and take a look."

"No," said Dee, slowly. "I think that might be a very bad idea."

Eli looked at her, expectantly.

Dee started to shrug, then snorted and shook her head. "Look. I'm not saying this makes any sense."

"What do you know, Dee?"

"I don't know that I know anything. It's just ... how does the house feel to you tonight, Eli?"

"Feel?" Eli ran his lips around the way Mom did when she was nervous. "Right now I don't know. But it felt good earlier. I was going to stay awake and listen for footsteps—"

"But you were too relaxed, right? You just drifted off to sleep before you knew it?"

Eli nodded.

"But it doesn't feel as good right now, does it?"

"Not ... quite."

More scratching at the wall. Eli and Dee listened in silence.

"Something's trying to get in, Eli. Something that was in the attic isn't now. And it wants back inside."

"Some*thing*?"

Dee nodded.

"But it's outside now. It can't just come back in."

"I don't think so." Dee shook her head. "I hope not."

Eli sighed, rolled his shoulders and neck. "Look, out there is safer than in the attic. And nothing really happened when ... whatever it is was in the attic. So we should get some sleep."

Dee nodded. Eli gave her a hug and started back for his room. But before he got through her doorway, Dee got his attention back.

"Hey. Do you think Mom really met with a contractor?"

Eli shrugged. "Whatever she did, let's hope it worked."

INTERVIEW SNIPPET

Excerpt from 1996 interview with Barclay "Bones" McElroy

Yeah, I'll admit free of charge. When I saw that young priest go over there, I started thinking that maybe this family would be all right after all. I mean, a family with that much love, that's gotten right with the Man Upstairs?

That just sounded to me like the perfect recipe to take care of whatever it is that ails that house. What's that word they use in the big cities? Gentrify? You know, when they take a bad place and they make it good? You see it in the paper sometimes.

You know, I'm answering all your questions. The least you could do is answer a few of mine. Kids today. No respect for your elders.

Anyway, I figured that young priest was a good sign. I figured that maybe this was just the right family to gentrify the place, make it habitable for decent folks again.

And I didn't hear anything that night. Didn't even see so much as the glow of a flashlight. Got so relaxed my own self that I turned in no later than about two Ack Emma. Thought maybe I could ease back on my vigil. Thought that maybe this time would be different.

Well, I guess you know that's not how it played out. Otherwise you wouldn't be here asking me questions.

But for that one night, at least, that house was quiet. Yessir.

Goes to show though. The Man Upstairs, He can only help as much as His own vessels here on earth are willing and able to let Him through. I don't know, I'm just saying that maybe that priest wasn't as holy as he might've been. Maybe he was thinking impure thoughts about that pretty Mrs. Dumas.

Or maybe they just should have left Rome out of it entirely and gone to a good Lutheran minister, like the one who's been preaching the Gospel at my church for two decades *plus* some change.

Longer than that priest of theirs had been alive, the day he came over to do whatever it is he did.

That's all I'm saying. I think they had the right idea. I just think they must've gone to the wrong man. The way things worked out.

(at this point, Mr. McElroy crossed himself)

4

Wednesday June 14th, 1989. Day Three.

"Daddy?"

Lex's head was pounding like he'd gone ten rounds with the champ. He had to force his eyes open, and the morning sunshine was way, way too bright.

Lex was lying down, but he wasn't in bed.

Why ... where ...

Suddenly his eyes found their focus and his surroundings made sense.

He was in the living room, stretched out on the brown sectional in front of the red brick fireplace. He was wearing his tartan bathrobe over his boxers. His mouth tasted like an ashtray, but not as moist. His skin felt grungy all over, like maybe he *had* gotten into a boxing match — which would at least explain the headache — and then just collapsed afterwards.

Hadn't he dreamed something about a boxing match? Something about the champion with the pale skin and a red scar...

"Daddy?"

Lex shook his head. Regretted it immediately, but the rest of the room clicked into place. The boxes next to the coffee table. He could hear swallows in the yard through an open window — that was bringing in a pleasant breeze — and Gina whisking something in the kitchen, talking in a soft voice.

And right in front of him stood Ava, in her astronaut pajamas, her long black hair tied back in a ponytail.

Lex forced a smile across his face. "G..." He had to clear his throat twice before he could muster enough saliva to croak, "Good morning, sweetie."

"You okay, Daddy? You stink."

He did? Lex sniffed the air, but if he stank he couldn't tell. Not that it made a difference. And no, he definitely wasn't okay. That ashtray taste — where did that come from? Lex never smoked a day in his life. And the way his head pounded, like a bad hangover maybe. But Lex didn't drink last night. And why did he feel so grungy?

He cleared his throat a few more times, until he could almost sound human.

"Yeah, baby," he said, sitting up slowly. "Your daddy's okay. Just needs a shower." And a gallon of orange juice and about a thousand aspirin.

Ava put her hand on his forehead. Jerked her hand back.

"Mom!" she yelled, turning and running toward the kitchen. "Daddy's got a fever."

The whisking stopped. He heard Gina issue a few orders to whoever was in the kitchen with her, then the whisking resumed as Gina padded into the living room.

Gina was dressed. Lime green slacks and a pretty white sleeveless blouse. Still barefoot though. She smelled like lilacs this morning.

Lex wasn't sure what kind of greeting to expect after last night, but she had that little worry crease between her eyebrows.

"Phew," she said, waving her hand in the air. "Dig a ditch last night before you turned in?" She put her hand on his forehead. Sighed. "Shower for you, mister, and aspirin. Then bed. I'll bring your breakfast in later."

"What about—"

But she must have known what he was going to say, because she gave a dismissive wave. "We'll discuss that later too. Don't want you saying later that I took advantage of a sick man's bad judgment."

Back to the kitchen she went.

Lex leaned forward, elbows on his knees. He was tired. Bone tired. Tired as though he hadn't slept at all. And sore, as though if he hadn't been boxing, he had to have been digging.

No blisters on his fingers or raw spots on his hands. No bruising or tearing on his knuckles. Probably not boxing or digging in his sleep then. That much was good.

Still. He must have done something.

Did people spontaneously start sleepwalking?

Lex ran his fingers over his face as he thought. Even his stubble ached.

His stubble ached? No. That just meant his skin was extra sensitive for some reason. The fever, maybe. Everywhere he touched — hands, face, neck — ached like his nerves were too close to the surface. And maybe it was just the power of suggestion, but he *could* smell himself now, and apart from the sweat stink he detected something like ham.

"You better not still be in the living room," said Gina in a loud, singsong voice.

Lex dragged himself to his feet. Why so much effort?

Why was the room spinning...

Lex grabbed the arm of the couch, but fell anyway.

Thump

"Ow. Ow. Ow." He kept repeating it. The cherry hardwood was much less comfortable than the couch. He'd landed hard on his back. Bonked his head too. All those too-close-to-the-surface nerves jangling pain every which way. He supposed he was lucky he didn't clip the edge of the coffee table. The way the room kept spinning.

"Dad?" Mason was there. Jean shorts and a cropped yellow-and-black jersey shirt. He was so much more handsome than Lex had been at his age. Must must have gotten all the best genes from both his parents...

"Dad!"

Strong too, the way he hoisted Lex's shoulders. But his hands were cold. And why was he tugging down on Lex's cheek with one finger? Why was he staring into Lex's eyes like that?

Why was the room so cold?

Lex's teeth started chattering.

"Eli! Give your brother a hand." Gina's in-charge voice. Sweet, brilliant Gina. Why did her family tap dance on her head about God like that? "Get him to the bedroom. Dee get the bathtub running. Tepid. You hear? Tepid."

"Tepid," came Dee's answer, and Lex could hear bare feet running down the hall.

Lex could see Eli now. Basketball shorts and a plain white tee. Eli. Poor kid. Second born and second place. Forever in big brother's shadow, clinging there with his twin sister.

Strong though. Strong enough to carry Lex's legs while Mason hefted Lex by the shoulders.

The hallway spun in cherry circles while Lex rocked down the hall in the arms of his eldest boys.

The walls ... needed ... paint...

At least that nice Mr. McElroy — Bones — across the street was as good as his word. Not a doctor, true, but when Lex collapsed Gina wasn't even sure where their insurance was good down here. Or even if Briar had a hospital at all.

Turns out it did. Bones knew it well. About fifteen minutes from the house.

But Bones also said Lex didn't need the hospital.

When Byron ran to fetch him, Bones came over without a hint of complaint. Checked Lex over twice. Asked a few questions, then pronounced that it was just a flu. Same sort of thing he'd seen a dozen times if he'd seen it once. Came on "all sudden like" but he should be fine.

And if, by evening, Gina wanted a second opinion, he was willing to help get Lex to the hospital. Knew what calls to make and which nurses to talk to.

Now Gina sat on their bathroom counter in her lime green pants and simple white bra, legs folded underneath her on the white marble between her sink and Lex's. Her blouse hung on the robe hook on the back of the bathroom door, so she didn't get it wet while she washed her sleeping husband.

She looked down at Lex in the bathtub. The water had to be too cold by now. He'd been in there more than twenty minutes, just soaking after she scrubbed most of the areas she could reach. So much dried, salty sweat. What had he been doing?

She had her little dishes of lavender potpourri next to his head, so he had something more pleasant to smell than soap and water.

That water *had* to be too cold. He was shivering now, lids twitching like he was dreaming. She should either add some more hot water or get him out of there.

But she couldn't lift Lex herself, and she really didn't want to make Mason and Eli do it again. The little ones were scared enough without watching their big brothers carry their unconscious father twice in one day.

Gina should probably be out there with her children right now. Not leaving the eldest three to watch the youngest. Mason, Eli and Dee were probably just as scared as Bryon, Ava, and Roy.

As scared as Gina had been herself.

But she couldn't bring herself to leave her husband just yet.

She couldn't let him keep sleeping there though, either. He'd prune away to nothing.

Gina hopped down off the counter. She stuck her hand into the cool water and flipped the stopper to drain the tub. The water started its whirlpool, and she could hear it begin rushing away down the pipes.

She leaned in and kissed Lex's forehead. Still so hot. Was the aspirin doing anything?

She wouldn't wait for evening. If he wasn't looking any better by noon, he was going to the hospital.

She patted his cheek softly, but rapidly.

"Hon? Lex? Can you hear me?"

A low sound, somewhere between a groan and a growl. He turned his head away.

Well, at least that was a response.

"Come on, honey. Can you wake up for Gina?"

He twitched, and groaned a little more. His eyes were really going behind his eyelids now. Must've been having a heck of a dream. His arms started twitching too, like he was doing something in the dream. Fighting the fever, maybe.

She patted his face again, maybe a half-dozen times. Then another half-dozen, harder.

"Lex, honey, wake up. You're having a bad dream."

Still nothing, except that he started making little sounds. Frightened sounds.

"I'm sorry, honey," she said, and slapped him hard.

His eyes snapped open, pupils so wide she could barely see the green surrounding them.

"Huh! Huh. Huh." He was blinking fast, and flinching.

"Lex? Can you hear me? Lex?"

"G-G-G-Gina?"

She leaned in and slipped her arms around him. His wet skin was so hot. Bones had measured his temperature at one-oh-two-point-three and declared that it was high but not dangerous. She wanted to take it again.

But not right now. Right now she just wanted to hold him while he shook.

His hands came around her then, weakly hugging her back.

"You know," she said, trying to sound playful, "this isn't fair at all. I had a good mad going and you had to spoil it by getting sick."

"S-s-s-so c-c-c-cold."

"Can you sit up, honey? I'll get your robe."

But he wouldn't let go. He just squeezed harder. She reached up and stroked his wet, sandy blonde hair. "Shhh," she said. "I've got you, honey. We'll just dry you off. Then we'll get you into your pajamas and your robe and put you to bed."

"L-l-l-love y-y-y-you."

"I love you too, honey."

She managed to extract herself then, and helped Lex towel himself dry. She ran the towel over her wet front as well, and lamented that she'd have to change her now-wet bra too. But she fetched the striped pajamas he only ever wore when her parents were visiting, and came back in to see Lex huddled around himself, hands between his thighs for warmth.

Her heart lurched at the sight. He just looked so sad and pathetic she wanted to wrap him in a blanket and give him cocoa and read to him.

Getting him into the pajamas and robe took longer than she expected, but finally he was sitting, half-asleep, on the edge of the tub and she was tying closed his robe. He was still shivering.

"Come on, honey," she said, helping him to his feet. But then his whole weight all but collapsed on her. "*Oof.*"

She managed to keep him steady. More or less. Though she was sweating from the effort herself by the time she finally got him between the sheets. And by the time she tucked him in he was fast asleep again. Still shivering.

It wasn't enough. But it was all she could think to do right now. Especially since it seemed to her that he should have felt too *hot*, not too *cold*. What with a fever like that. But Bones said some people react differently to fevers, and Gina just couldn't remember how Lex had been, the last time he had a high fever.

He got sick so rarely.

Gina changed her bra — drying off her front one more time before she dressed again. And she left the bedroom door open when she went back down the hall to check on the kids.

They were all sitting around the dining room table, Mason leading the whole crew in a game of hangman. Not that any of them sounded as though their hearts were in it. And every head snapped her direction the moment she entered the room.

"Your father's fine," she lied. "He must have caught something in Monterey yesterday. Any of you feeling under the weather? Any chills or aches?"

Roy was the last to shake his head, brow furrowed as though he really had to think about it. But none of them admitted to having any symptoms. So far, so good.

"What did he eat? Maybe this is food poisoning."

"Same as the rest of us," said Mason. "Fish and chips from a busy little place on the docks."

"Did he have a beer with it maybe?"

"Nope. Soda like the rest of us. Eruption, I think."

Eruption Cola seemed harmless enough.

"He had some of the taffy," said Ava.

"Right," said Mason. "We all shared a bag of salt water taffy."

Gina snorted. "No wonder I still have half a lasagna in the fridge."

"What about you, Mom?" said Dee, her gaze piercing.

"I'm fine," Gina said, waving a dismissive hand. "I don't seem to have caught whatever your father has." Though she certainly gave him a chance to infect her while the kids were out last night. She drew a deep breath. "All right, you guys keep your game going. I'll get the thermometer and we'll go around the room."

Gina started with herself, to forestall any complaints. Everyone had normal temperatures. Even under further questioning, not one of the kids would admit to feeling any aches or chills. Whatever Lex had, it was only troubling him. That was something, at least.

Byron won the game of hangman. As usual. Gina wondered if there were any games that boy *didn't* excel at.

"All right," she said. "Back to unpacking everyone. We have a lot to do. Don't worry about your father, I'll keep an eye on him and give you all a report with lunch."

They scattered slowly, but they went, bonging their way up that wrought iron spiral staircase. Busy work would do them good. Keep their hands and minds occupied. Keep them from worrying about their father.

Just as well. Gina would worry enough for all of them.

Eli sat on the floor of his room, surrounded by the same stacks of books that he'd managed to ignore last night after that trip to Monterey.

Well, not quite the same. After more than an hour's work — helped along by Tesla's *The Great Radio Controversy* playing on his boom box — he finally had them organized in piles that made sense to him. Piles that could be easily transferred to the shelves. Once he decided which ones went where.

His windows were open, letting in a little air via the warm morning breeze, along with the smell of cedar trees and begonias. He preferred the cedar, of course. Still. And Eli would never admit this to anyone. Well, maybe except Dee, but this was one of the things she'd know without him telling her anyway.

Eli liked the smell of the begonias too.

There was something cheerful about it. And after that scare with Dad this morning, cheerful was a good thing. Seeing Dad collapsed on the living room floor like that — that had taken all the taste out of the Eli's bacon-and-scrambled-eggs breakfast. But Bones swore up and down that Dad would be okay, and Bones sounded like he knew what he was talking about.

Still, Eli would sooner die than admit to Mason that he liked the smell of a flower.

Eli arranged his basketball books on the shelf just under his compact discs. There weren't enough to spread across the whole two bookshelves, but he had a couple of swimming books too. And one about fencing, which he hoped to take up someday. If Mason didn't. He'd already ruined judo, which killed Eli's interest in all the Asian martial arts.

Eli was just trying to decide if his handful of books about World War II planes would make sense next to the book on fencing when Dee poked her head in.

"*Jinkatha*," she said. *Something's wrong.*

The hairs on the back of Eli's neck stood up. He looked up at her.

She'd dressed to mirror him. Soccer shorts instead of basketball, but a plain white tee shirt. And she had that worried look in her eyes.

"*Fafa neefa*," he said, voice low. That one didn't have a direct translation. It was like "hush" and "not so loud" and "come closer to say that" and a couple of other things, all rolled into one. And all of them telling her to speak English, because Mom or Mason might be listening.

He nodded toward his bed, and Dee quick-stepped to it and tucked her feet under her as she sat. Eli didn't have to say anything. Just looked at Dee and waited for her to talk.

"Something's been bugging me all morning, but I just now realized what."

Eli raised his eyebrows.

"Did you notice the window downstairs?"

"No."

"It was open."

Eli looked at the two open windows on the wall behind where Dee sat, then back at his twin.

"No," she said, "I mean it was open when we came downstairs this morning. As in maybe Dad opened it *last night*."

"The scratches," Eli said, scratching the back of his neck. "You think Dad let in whatever was scratching at the walls?"

"And now Dad's sick. I mean passed out sick."

"You think something bit him?" But as soon as the question was past his lips, Eli was already shaking his head. "No, Mom or Bones would have seen the bite mark."

Eli's eyes widened. They got so wide he could feel them dry out. She didn't think...

Eli looked at Dee and didn't have to ask the question. He knew what she was thinking. It was the same thing he suggested the other day.

"Ghosts."

"Ghosts," she said, nodding. "I think you were right the other day, and I'm sorry I laughed at you. I think we've got a ghost, Eli."

"So what do we do about it?"

A sigh exploded out of her. "I thought *you* knew! You're the one always reading those sci-fi and fantasy books."

"That's *fiction*, Dee. Fiction. I don't exactly have any books about ghosts..."

Eli flashed on Mason, reading that Clive Barker book on the drive to Monterey yesterday. Big brother had always had a darker taste in books than Eli...

"But you know who might?"

Once more, Eli didn't have to answer his own question. One moment of eye contact and he and Dee were on the same page. They said it in unison.

"Mason."

DEE KNEW SHE HAD TO TAKE THE LEAD IN THIS CONVERSATION. THERE was no way Eli could broach the subject of ghosts. Not with Mason. Whether Mason believed in them or not, he would tease Eli mercilessly for even asking the question. She was sure of it.

This seemed like it fell into the category of those things about boys that Dee was never going to understand. Not even as close as she was to Eli. *Him* she could understand. But once Eli started speaking *boy* with Mason or some kid at school, Dee just couldn't follow it. Boys had mysteries and systems of priorities and communication that she could never hope to crack.

She would just have to hope that Mason wouldn't be as rough on his baby sister as he'd be on his younger brother.

She led the way, their feet hushing on the hallway hardwood while strains of Weird Al's *Dare to Be Stupid* came from Byron's room.

She stood in the doorway to Mason's room, Eli just behind her. The door was open this time — and so were both of Mason's windows, above his bureau and bookcase...

Wait. Was he *all unpacked?*

His bookshelf was full of books, even across the top where he used baseball trophies as bookends. More baseball and football trophies on his bureau, and the one trophy he kept from his two-year flirtation with judo at the start of high school. Trophies everywhere that wasn't taken up by his small stack of CDs, his small black boom box, and that carved wooden box he kept all his necklaces in.

Dee never understood Mason and his necklaces. He must have had fifty, most of them gifts from girlfriends. And he wore one every day. But he always wore them tucked into his shirt, so that only a little bit of the chain was showing, if that.

Dee just couldn't understand. Why wear them at all if he was going to hide them away like that? Must've been another boy thing.

The door to his closet was open, and she could see clothes and bits of uniforms hanging. On the floor in front of the closet, a pile of about a dozen boxes, all broken down flat.

Mason himself was flopped on his maroon-and-tan striped bedspread — which contrasted horribly with his yellow-and-black cropped jersey shirt — reading a paperback.

Shock at the tableau before her changed the question that came out of Dee's mouth.

"Are you *seriously unpacked already*?"

"I don't spend all my time huddled in some corner speaking a private language." Mason looked up. "Honestly, you could both accomplish so much more if you just had a little motivation."

"*Kathika a ta atha*," muttered Eli. *I hate him sometimes.*

Dee nodded, but what she said was, "What do you think's wrong with Dad?"

"Flu." Mason looked from Dee to Eli and back again, then sighed and marked his place in the book with his finger. "Come on in, guys."

Mason sat up, his pillows cushioning his back against the wall. Dee and Eli sat on opposite corners of his bed. Mason rated a queen-size bed too. Dee and Eli were both stuck with full-size.

"I get it," Mason said. "I'm worried about him too. But Mom's doing everything she can to keep his temperature down, and there's nothing a hospital could do for him, really, unless he starts having trouble keeping down fluids. Then he might need an I.V. or something."

"Hit him pretty sudden though," said Eli.

"Flus do that sometimes."

"And none of *us* got it?" said Dee. "Not even the snotmonsters?"

Not the kindest nickname for Ava and Roy, but she didn't use it often, and as far as she was concerned they'd more than earned it. Those two brought home more illnesses from school, each, than Mason, Eli, Dee and Byron had brought home combined. They were like sickness magnets, those two.

Mason shrugged. "Even those two can't catch *everything*. I mean, that's simple probability, isn't it?"

Eli and Dee looked at each other. He was about to use the g-word, but in the flash of contact Dee managed to persuade him not to. She could feel him agree to let her take the lead.

"What if ... what if it's not a flu?"

Mason looked back and forth between Eli and Dee. "Just what do you have in mind?"

"Did you hear any footsteps last night?"

"No," he said slowly, drawing out the word as though really asking *what are you getting at?* "Mom's contractor took care of that."

"Did you hear *anything* strange last night?"

Mason narrowed his eyes. "Like what?"

"Like scratches," said Bryon, standing in Mason's doorway. "They want to know if you heard something scratching at the walls, like it was trying to get in."

Byron had on some cut-off jean shorts like Mason, but a Weird Al tee shirt. Those were his comfort clothes, Dee knew. He wore them like armor when something was bugging him.

"That's what I heard anyway." Bryon walked in without waiting for Mason's invitation. He perched on the edge of the bed, midway between Eli and Dee. "I'm guessing you guys heard the same?"

Dee and Eli both nodded.

"You guys do realize," said Mason, "that we're on the second floor. Right? I mean, you all took the steps to get here—"

"We *heard* it, Mason," said Dee.

Eli nodded. Byron looked back and forth between them, then looked at Mason expectantly.

"Tree branches," said Mason. "We probably have to trim back the cedars or something."

"I looked out the window," said Byron. "No tree branches close enough to make that sound."

"Did you open the window?" said Dee, trying to sound casual.

"I'm not an idiot," said Byron.

"So did you see anything? Making the scratches, I mean."

Byron shook his head.

Mason sighed. "Then I hate to say it, but it sounds to me like we've got rats in the walls. Must have been disturbed by the work of Mom's contractor, and probably scuttled about all night trying to build a new nest. We'll have to get an exterminator or something."

"You actually buy that bullshit about a contractor?" said Byron, and when the swear word left his mouth Dee felt her eyes go wide.

Mason snapped his fingers aggressively. "You want me to tell Mom and Dad about the kind of language you're using?"

"What are you getting at, Byron?" said Eli.

"I'm just trying to say what you two are dancing around." Byron threw up his hands. "Ghosts. There. It's out there on the table. Now—"

"Annnd let's take it right back off the table," said Mason.

"Why?" said Dee.

Mason dog-eared a page in his book and slapped it against his thigh.

"Ghosts aren't real, dum-dums. Those 'footsteps' were boards that needed tightening. That 'scratching' is probably rats. And Dad's got the flu. That's it."

"Who says ghosts aren't real?" said Byron.

"Oh, I don't know." Mason mockingly scratched his forehead. "Oh. Yeah. *Every scientist ever.*" He held up his book, *Cabal* by Clive Barker. "This is where ghosts belong. Not out here. And not" — he reached over and tapped Byron on the forehead — "in here."

"Whatever," said Byron, hopping off the bed and heading for the doorway.

Dee glanced over at Mason's bookshelf. Apart from the football and baseball books she saw author names like Stephen King, Peter Straub, Robert McCammon, James Herbert, Brian Lumley... All horror authors. But no actual books about ghosts or the supernatural.

"Guys," said Mason, pitched lower so Byron couldn't hear, "you need to knock this off. Now. Bryon's not likely to bring it up again on his own, so let this be the end of it before Ava and Roy overhear and start getting nightmares."

Dee and Eli looked at each other. He didn't look any more convinced than she felt.

"That's another thing," said Mason. "You need to give this" — he pointed back and forth between them — "a break. It's creepy, and frankly the more you do it the more trouble you'll have dealing with people who aren't you two."

Eli's cheeks reddened with shame.

No. Not now. Not with all this going on.

Eli got up and strode from the room.

Dee could feel her mouth hang open. Could feel herself blink slowly.

Eli was always so worried about Mason's opinion. Even when he didn't want to be. But ... he wouldn't really cut himself off from Dee. Not now, of all times.

"It's better this way," said Mason. "I mean, it's good that you're close, but there's such a thing as too close. You know?"

But Dee didn't know that. She didn't know that at all.

GINA FELT AS THOUGH SHE SPENT HER WHOLE MORNING RUNNING around. And with the day warming up as it was, all this running around had her sweating...

"Glistening." She could almost hear her mother insist the word was "glistening" when it came to women. "Only men *sweat*" she'd said a million times. "Women glisten."

Well, Gina was "glistening" enough that she was itching under her breasts. She'd need a shower by mid-afternoon, if she could spare the time.

At least all the windows were open now, and pretty much every direction she went she got a little breeze and a smell of begonias.

And every direction just about summed up her morning.

Down the hall to check on Lex. Up the stairs to check on the kids. Circle back past to double-check Byron, Ava and Roy and make sure they were all right after the morning's shock. Then back down the stairs to get at least a few things put away and organized before the cycle started again.

Not much change, as far as Lex went. He couldn't seem to handle ice packs. He was shivering even without them, and she couldn't bring herself to push the issue too hard. She had to settle for re-wetting a wash cloth with each trip and laying it across his forehead.

Of course, it was gone half the time, when she came into the room. Thrown off in his tossing and turning. He was sleeping, that much was sure, but she wished he'd sleep like a rock. Get the kind of deep, restful sleep Gina associated with what the body needed to heal itself.

Instead, it was like he was dreaming nonstop. Eyes rolling behind his lids. Sweat on his brow and soaking his robe. Twitching and shifting about in fits and starts. Groaning and half-muttering words she couldn't make out.

Whatever fever dream he was having, it was a doozy.

She'd tried different configurations of pillows, blankets and sheets, but nothing she did seemed to help.

He could take water though, at least, when she tilted his head up and eased some between his lips. Just a little at a time, but he never choked on it, and she'd seen no signs that he might vomit. She'd even gotten him to swallow some scrambled eggs earlier, though the bacon was too scratchy for his raw throat.

Gina didn't understand why his throat was so raw, either. He hadn't been coughing...

Anyway, if he could just stay awake longer, she might make him suck on some eucalyptus lozenges. Maybe that would help. But he had so much trouble staying awake, even trying the lozenges might not be safe.

The last thing she'd want would be to make him choke.

But he'd have to eat something for lunch. Had to keep his strength up.

She'd have to wake him up again, after she fed the kids their lunch. Get him to eat a little soup. As long as he could do at least that much. As long as he could keep replenishing his liquids and getting some nutrition, then his body could fight and he wouldn't have to go to the hospital.

That was what Bones told her anyway. And Gina clung to that idea. Carting her husband off to the hospital would…

No. She needed to focus on the positive right now, not play out disaster scenarios in her head. That was her mother's way. Gina needed to focus on what she knew, what she could do.

Upstairs the kids seemed to be doing all right. More or less. Calming down after their morning fright.

Mason was Mason, of course. Already unpacked, with a promise that he'd check on Ava and Roy sometimes too, to make sure Gina got to spend more time seeing to Lex. All his baseball posters up — Giants and A's, and couple of players from outside the Bay Area, ones Gina should probably have recognized — plus that Heather Thomas poster. Pink bikini, hot tub, enough to make any mother sigh.

The swimsuit calendar didn't get to her. But the Heather Thomas poster. That one looked like the kind of girl she most wanted Mason to avoid. The kind who could get him into trouble. He just *had* to bring that poster with him in the move.

Maybe he'd take it with him off to college. Then, at least, she wouldn't have to see it…

Gina was half-tempted to assign Mason a few downstairs boxes to unpack, but no. He deserved a little reward for finishing his boxes first, and if he wanted to laze and read a little that was fine with her. Especially since he'd promised to keep an eye on Ava and Roy.

Dee was moping a bit, making not much more than desultory

attempts at unpacking. Her posters were still rolled up in one corner, and most of her boxes not even cut open yet. She had a few clothes, at least, in a couple of open drawers, and her jewelry box on top of the dresser, but that looked like about it. Even her desk was bare except for one sketch pad and an open pack of pencils.

She'd been sketching. That was good. Therapeutic and all her own, something she didn't share with Eli.

Still, honestly, if she didn't step up her unpacking, that girl will still be living out of boxes when school starts. It wasn't worry about her father, either. Dee was like Gina in the way she handled worry — she got more active. Worry might have gotten Dee entirely unpacked by now.

So she had to have been sulking about something else. Missing Sebastian, perhaps, but that couldn't be helped. Wasn't good for a girl her age to get too serious about a boy anyway.

Gina would have to have a talk with her about Sebastian. After dinner maybe. Tell her about Jimmy, so she'd know her mother *does* know a little bit about heavy high school crushes.

God, she hoped Dee hadn't gone as far with Sebastian as Gina had with Jimmy.

Gina would have to ask a few delicate questions before telling the story. Just in case. No reason to give the girl ideas.

Eli had his posters up too. Basketball, basketball, basketball, and the naked whore with the guitar. Eli claimed the whore could play that guitar. But if that were true, then why couldn't she have been dressed? And holding it? Why did she have to be naked and lying down, with the guitar strategically arranged in front of her?

Gina had considered just throwing that poster away at least a dozen times, but always let Lex talk her out of it. Lex seemed to think the poster was a healthy thing for a boy Eli's age. Of course, Lex's freshman-year college roommate had kept even worse pictures on the wall beside his bed...

Anyway, Eli seemed to be making headway with his books, but he was sulking about something too. Didn't even have any of his music going, and that wasn't like him at all.

Could have been worried about his father, of course, but Gina wondered. He might have been picking up on whatever was bothering Dee. Those two were like that.

Or maybe he was disappointed that he didn't hear any ghostly footsteps in the attic last night. Boys could be like that too, she knew. Fascinated with things that didn't make sense.

Gina smiled. Well, if that was his problem, he'd have to get over it. Father Andrew had sent the ghost packing and Gina never needed to see that ... pale face ... or that red scar...

She shivered and crossed herself.

Baptisms all around. Yes. Lex would agree. She'd see to it. Then they'd be safe. Then that ghost could never come back.

Faith was armor, like Father Andrew said. And Gina had every intention of seeing to it that her children were well protected.

Byron's room already looked like Byron's room. His cassette player and Weird Al tapes were on the bureau — playing, of course, and Gina had never realized before that accordion music could qualify as "raucous" — and his clothes and books were scattered across the floor. If he'd had his Weird Al poster up and his model airplanes hanging from the ceiling, it would look just like his half of the room he'd shared with Roy back in Sunnyvale.

Byron was curled up on a clear spot of hardwood, surrounded by a haphazard array of books, nose deep in a hardback he'd picked up at some library book sale. Byron was a fiend for library book sales. Most eclectic reader Gina'd ever seen. No pattern she could pick out to what he'd pick up and what he wouldn't. History, folklore, fiction, poetry. Sometimes she thought he just opened each book at random and started reading.

A few well-chosen words pried him out of his book and got him started on getting the clothes and books from the floor to the bureau and bookcase, respectively. He'd just throw his clothes into drawers, too, but at least they wouldn't get walked on.

This accomplished, Gina continued on.

Ava might have needed help, but she'd never admit it. Incredible focus, that one, when she had her mind on a task. Right now she was arranging her collection of seashells *just so* across her bureau, watching the way they caught the light and decided which looked prettiest.

The prettiest would go on the window sill. That was established Ava policy, and just about the only girly thing she liked. Otherwise, right now, her life was all space and astronauts. Her high-powered telescope was in one corner, already unpacked and waiting for the coming weekend, when Lex had promised to help her pick the best spot in the back yard for stargazing. Ten years old and already talking about orbital velocities and the likelihood that she could someday be the first woman to set foot on Mars.

Gina wondered if this interest would hold, the way soccer seemed to be so far. But only last year Ava had been all about the seas, not the skies, and the year before that ... football. Yes. Ava had noticed that there were no girls on Mason's football team and determined to become the first girl to play in the NFL.

Gina could not thank God hard enough that Ava had moved on from that one.

Arranging her seashells all morning was not the most productive way Ava could be spending her time, but every step she took to make the room her own was a good one, as far as Gina was concerned. So Gina didn't do much more than kiss her daughter and offer praise about the arrangement before moving on.

Roy had gotten distracted again. Gina knew that before she reached his room. She could hear the beeping and booping.

Sure enough, when Gina reached Roy's door, he was sitting in the middle of his unmade twin bed, staring at the tiny L.E.D. screen of a handheld electronic basketball game while his thumbs worked furiously. The game was ... Eli's or Mason's, Gina couldn't remember which, but Roy seemed to have claimed it as a hand-me-down since the original owner had lost interest.

Roy's boxes were all cut open, and Gina could see that at least some clothes had been dumped without ceremony into open dresser drawers. Underwear and tee-shirts and socks, all mixed together.

Gina sighed. She'd have to re-arrange the whole thing. Or maybe

... maybe Roy was old enough now that she could make him do it. Just tell him where everything went, and content herself with checking his work.

Unlike Gina's other children, Roy had no books unpacked yet. Reading had not yet taken with this one. Roy was always happier doing than reading, no matter what the book or what the activity. He'd sooner throw a tennis ball against the wall and make a game of catching it than sit still long enough to read one of the picture books he'd loved so much when Gina or Lex were reading to him.

Gina didn't interrupt him. Roy would have had questions about his father, and the only good answers would have been lies.

After lunch. After lunch she'd get Lex to eat some soup. Get some better news to report. Then she could get Roy started on repairing the unpacking he'd already done, and maybe moving on from there.

After lunch.

BY A COUPLE OF HOURS AFTER LUNCH — CHICKEN SOUP FROM CANS AND peanut-butter-and-raspberry-jelly sandwiches — Eli had his books put away. He even had his clothes either hanging in his closet or stuffed into his dresser.

That mostly left arranging his Star Wars toys, and Eli just couldn't get interested enough to do that right now. Normally he would have set up his stormtroopers and tusken raiders in a firefight with Han, Chewie, Lando, and Princess Leia while Luke was locked in a lightsaber battle with Darth Vader. Obi-Wan and Yoda would be positioned somewhere that they could look on.

Right now, the toys didn't feel like fun. They felt childish. Eli even had an urge to offer his TIE fighter and X-wing to Byron, but he was smart enough not to do that. Not right now. Not with so much going on.

Eli just sat there on his bed, in silence, and stared at his sole unpacked box. Star Wars toys. His Starting Lineup basketball figures: Michael Jordan (two of those, one up for a dunk and one dribbling),

Larry Bird, and Ralph Sampson and Chris Mullin of the Warriors. And a copy of Statis-Pro Basketball, the board game he'd found while in a thrift store with Byron but never gotten around to trying out.

How many other things had Eli not gotten around to trying? How many things had he given up because he was "too close" to Dee? How many people?

But Dee wasn't just his sister. She was his twin. How could they possibly be too close?

But Mason said they were. And Mason was, well, Mason. He had the worst trait possible in an older brother. He seemed to be right about everything.

But could Mason be wrong about this one?

It wasn't as though he could understand. It wasn't as though Mason could feel Dee's sadness across the hall. It wasn't as though Mason had the urge to go to her, to reassure her, to comfort her. Mason couldn't feel these things because he couldn't *feel* her the way Eli could. So he didn't really understand. And if he didn't really understand, he couldn't be right.

Could he?

He was still Mason...

Eli dropped back onto his bed and sighed. Warm cedar-scented air came in on the afternoon breeze. If June was this hot, August was going to be a bear.

This was no good. Sitting here was no good. Worrying about Mason's opinion was no good. Feeling Dee's sadness — especially without going to her — that was worse than no good. Plus Dad was sick, and Mom was starting to fray at the edges, the way she was running around.

Eli had to get out of here.

And there was a basketball court not two blocks away.

Eli yanked on his sneakers and grabbed his basketball from the shelf in his closet.

Just the feel of the ball in his hands helped. The smell of the rubber, with added character from the residue of a thousand pick-up games. He gave it a couple of quick squeezes to check its pressure. Still good.

He tucked the ball under his arm and stepped over to Byron's room. Weird Al's album *Dare to Be Stupid* played at a reasonable volume, for once. Byron sat on the floor in the center of a mess of books. Three of them were open, only one of which was in his lap.

"Come shoot some," said Eli. "I need to get out of here for a few."

Byron looked at Eli, looked back at his books. Rolled his neck.

"Cool," he said, springing to his feet and grabbing his sneakers.

Eli led the way down the back stairs. He and Byron paused at the door to Mom and Dad's room, where Mom was putting a wet wash-cloth on Dad's forehead, and pulling back a soaked sheet. Dad's pajamas looked soaked too.

"How's he doing?" asked Eli.

Mom's neck darn near snapped, she looked up so fast. Took in the shoes and basketball in a single Mom-glance.

"Better," she said.

Eli had his doubts about that. Dad never seemed to stop moving. His legs were twitching, and his shoulders shifted about. His eyes were closed, but his brow furrowed and his lips were moving. Plus he was sweating and shivering at the same time, which didn't sound good to Eli at all.

Dad did not look any better. But saying that aloud would not have been Eli's smartest move. In fact, maybe this basketball idea was a bad one...

"Where are you two off to?" said Mom, tone sharp enough that Eli knew what his answer needed to be.

"Nowhere." Byron looked up at him, surprised, but Eli continued anyway. "I've got most of my stuff unpacked, so we were going to shoot some hoops, but maybe we shouldn't."

"No," said Mom, smiling, and Eli didn't like the smile. Looked fake, especially after that sharp tone. "You boys go ahead. Get some fresh air and exercise. Your father's ... your father's looking better. He may even be able to join us for dinner."

"I hope not," muttered Byron, but Eli didn't even look at him.

"You're sure?" Eli said.

"Go on, go ahead." Mom smiled again, and Eli felt a little chill down his back. "But Byron, I want all those books off your floor by the time you go to bed tonight."

"Yes, Ma'am," he said.

Byron was the first to move away from the door, but Eli was quick to follow. Not quick enough though. Byron sped like it was a walking race, and Eli had to hustle to keep up. Byron didn't slow down until they were out the door, on the sidewalk and halfway down the block.

Birds were singing out here, and Eli didn't recognize the songs. Must have been different birds than hung around in Sunnyvale. Down the street a professional gardener — the kind who wore head-phones while he worked — was mowing one of the big neighbor lawns with a big roaring mower. Must have gotten a lot of work on this block, because all the lawns were neat, but so far Eli'd only seen one other kid, and she wasn't asked to mow lawns.

But Eli had more immediate concerns than his neighbors' lawns.

He stopped Byron with a hand on the shoulder.

"What do you know?" demanded Eli.

"I don't—"

"I heard what you said, when Mom talked about Dad joining us for dinner. Why don't you want him to?"

"I'm not sure Dad's sick." Byron started walking again, and Eli kept pace. "Dad never gets sick, and when he does, he never gets sick like this."

"You think this has something to do with those scratches on the walls last night?"

Byron nodded. "I think Dad opened the window, and let some-thing in. And not just into the house. I think he let something into *him*, and he's fighting it like heck."

Wasn't any more than what Eli and Dee had already been guess-ing, but it sounded worse coming from Byron. More real, somehow. But...

"How do you know about this stuff?"

"I read a lot," said Byron, with a shrug. "Got a bunch of books about this stuff. Some Colin Wilson, and Cotton Mather, and Aleister Crowley..." Byron shook his head. "Man that guy sucks. Reading him is like ... like trying to read a bunch of words some dictionary just puked all over the page. Hard to make any sense of him. It's like he *didn't want* people to figure out what he was saying."

"Who is—"

"Colin Wilson's the best, though. Did you know people really cast spells and stuff? Real wizards and witches, not just in novels. He writes all about it. Richard Cavendish too, and some others."

"You think somebody cast a spell on Dad?"

Eli didn't try to keep the scorn out of his voice. He started bouncing the ball, dribbling between his knees with each step. Believing a house was maybe haunted was one thing. But witches and spells? Come on.

"Duh," said Byron, and he put his whole face into the word. "Of course not, stupid. Who'd want to hurt Dad?"

"Then what are you talking about?"

Byron gave Eli a look like Eli'd just smashed his favorite Weird Al tape with a hammer.

"Hey, you and Dee were the ones talking about ghosts first. And you asked me to come out here, like you wanted to talk without skeptic Mason overhearing. And you asked how I knew. And—"

"Hey, hey," said Eli, snatching the ball out of the air with one arm and holding up a halting hand with the other. He stopped walking and waited until Byron was looking at him.

Was Byron on the verge of tears? He was all red-faced.

"I'm sorry," Eli said. "I didn't mean—"

"It's not right. You and Mason strut around like Greek heroes, and *you've* always got Dee to talk to, but—"

"You can talk to me, Byron." Eli had to duck his head to meet his younger brother's eye. "Seriously. Anytime."

Byron was leaning away from him, jaw tucked and eyes narrowed like he was afraid.

"I mean it," Eli said firmly. "Anytime. Anything."

Eli held out his basketball.

"Come on," he said. "I'll teach you how to dribble so they can't steal it from you. And how to get space to shoot when they cover you. And *you* can start teaching *me* about this Colin Wilson stuff. You obviously know a lot more about it than I do."

Byron's face lit up as he took the ball.

***

DEE SAT CROSS-LEGGED ON HER WHITE COMFORTER, SKETCH PAD ON HER lap, looking out one of the two open windows behind her bed. She kneaded her putty rubber eraser rhythmically with the fingers of her left hand, and held her softest shading pencil in her right, poised and ready for final touches. Her hardest pencil was tucked behind her right ear, and the exact medium pencil behind her left.

She could hear a lawn mower going, somewhere down the block, and the distant honk of a car horn. But those things didn't matter. She couldn't draw them.

Her pencil box was open on the bed next to her, empty. Dee's other pencils were scattered on the bed in front of her.

The warm breeze blew into her face, and her eyes narrowed just a little as she stared hard at the leftmost cedar tree of the three in the side yard. This tree was the tallest, with a trunk she couldn't have put her arms around, and a tip taller than the telephone poles out front. Its branches must have spread fifteen or twenty feet from the trunk in places.

Back in Sunnyvale that would have put those branches through the window and halfway across the room she shared there with Ava. Here, they fell a good dozen feet shy of the wall.

Dee looked from the tree to her sketch pad. The neat grass looked right. The redwood fence with its knotholes and its dull-pointed boards and imperfectly level support beams looked right. The hints of the house next door looked right.

But the tree, it was still wrong. The branches were fine, even the two broken branches, and the tip of the top was bent at just the right angle. But the drawing was still off...

Something about the striations of the bark. Yes, it was close. And yes, maybe nobody would notice but her.

Still. It was wrong. Not good enough.

Drawing was good for her right now. Took focus. When Dee was drawing, she could just sink into the process and not worry about anything else. Yes, that included unpacking — which would piss Mom off to no end — but Dee needed that right now.

Stress over Dad, over Eli, over the possibility of a ghost, over the way Mom was looking frayed. Heck, over the move, over ... everything.

Dee needed a place, a mental space where she could be entirely herself and free. Drawing gave her that.

Eli didn't have drawing. That was why he wanted a guitar so bad. Eli could feel it when Dee sank into her art, could feel the way it helped her. Wanted something like that for himself, and he was sure — and so was Dee — that playing guitar could give him that.

Plus, Mason didn't play guitar.

Mom didn't understand any of that. Thought Eli's interest had something to do with girls, and maybe his Lita Ford poster. Maybe Dee could explain it when all this was over...

...if Mom would listen to her words, and not the fact that it was Dee saying them. Mom could get like that. So worried about how close Dee and Eli were...

A sob worked its way out of Dee, and she squeezed her putty rubber eraser out of shape. Why couldn't Mom leave them alone? Why couldn't Mason? They both got in Eli's head, and now he was trying to cut himself off from her again. Just like he had that awful summer two years ago, after the last time they'd had to see Dr. Clyburn.

Dee couldn't take that right now. Not with so much going on. She needed Eli. Needed her other half. And Eli needed her too. She knew it. There was no way they could...

Dee sighed through her nose. She dropped the shading pencil, picked up the middle hardness pencil, turned the page in her sketchbook, and started again.

This time she would get the striations right.

Dee sank into her work. She started with simple lines, faint, just enough to establish perspective and organize the space of the fresh sheet of paper. The barest bones of a skeleton that she would flesh out into her depiction of the tree.

Dee spent most of that afternoon with her sketchpad, getting further and further into her art. After the tree, she did all three trees. Then her two windows and the world outside them. Then she picked a spot between the leftmost tree and the center, a place where the branches crossed and overlapped. She started from the trunk of each tree — just enough of the trunk for perspective — then continued out along two branches from the left tree and one from the center. She drilled down into the details of the twigs and the tiny round leaves that were not quite needles. Thick enough that she could have pushed her thumbnail through them and felt the distance she pushed.

She even got the image of the boy sitting on the top branch of the three.

Wait. What boy?

Dee looked up again. No boy was sitting on that branch. She leaned forward to look down. Nobody was in her yard.

That was weird.

Dee looked back at her sketch pad. She'd definitely drawn a boy. Only a couple of years older than Roy, with tanned skin, short, messy brown hair and overalls with one suspender down. The knees of his overalls were patched, and he didn't have a shirt on under them.

Dee closed her eyes. Tried to picture the boy she must have seen when she drew him.

She couldn't call his image to mind. That was even weirder.

Dee didn't just look at things when she drew them. She drew them first in her head, then on the paper. And in her head they were always full color. She should have been able to see that boy in her head right now. Should have been able to recall if that spot on his left forearm was a shadow or a bruise.

But she had nothing.

She looked at the drawing again. The boy seemed to be looking right at her.

A chill ran through Dee, and she shivered. Was this the ghost? Was all of this — everything that was happening — some little dead boy who had business with the living?

She looked back at the branch where — according to her drawing — the boy had been sitting.

"Go away," she said. "Just leave us alone. Leave *my dad* alone. You're dead. It's our house now."

She sighed and closed her eyes.

"Just ... just go away."

"L*ex*?"

Gina sat on the bed beside her sick husband. She'd need to change these sweaty sheets, but he was getting better. Yes. She was sure he was getting better. His fever hadn't broken, but it was down. It was down a whole point since the last time she'd taken it. So maybe it wasn't broken, but it was breaking. Wasn't that how it worked?

Just twenty minutes ago Lex had still been holding steady at one-oh-two even, as he had most of the day.

As of five seconds ago, it was now one-oh-one even.

The ice packs must have been helping. And maybe fresh air from the open windows across the room, keeping the bedroom from getting stale with Lex's sweaty smells. Maybe even the songbirds outside, maybe they were helping too.

About an hour had passed since Gina finally put plastic bags of ice under his armpits, on his chest and on his forehead. Yes, Lex had shivered and tossed when she put them there, and whined in his sleep, but that fever *had* to come down. Between the fever and his sweating, her poor husband was practically steam-broiling himself.

And the fever *was* starting to come down. If the fever came down, the flu wasn't too serious. If the flu wasn't too serious, Lex didn't need to go to the hospital. That simple. Like math. Gina was always good at math.

She didn't seem to be as good at getting her children to unpack. Success rate running maybe fifty-fifty there. Mason was done, of course, and Eli was mostly done. Those two facts pushed Ava to get done too, because anything her big brothers could do, she could do.

Byron wasn't even close to done. Gina shouldn't have let him go play with Eli. What was she thinking?

Dee blew her afternoon drawing. Yes, she stopped and made small attempts to unpack when Gina forced her, but after the third time, Gina gave up for the day. And Roy with that electronic basketball game...

Gina couldn't do everything herself. She just couldn't.

And Lex was...

No. Lex was getting better. He was hardly twitching now. And Gina was sure he'd gotten some real sleep in there for a while this afternoon. Good sleep. Deep sleep. Not this weird, troubled dreaming he'd been doing most of the day.

Bones was right. Lex just needed time and fluids.

And a shower. All that sweating was making Lex — and his robe, pajamas, and these sheets — more than a little ripe. He might not have the strength to stand through it, what with spending all his energy to fight this flu, but Gina already had that part taken care of. It wasn't as though she could risk him in another bath. He might fall asleep and drown.

But first, he needed to wake up.

"Lex, hon? Can you wake up for Gina?"

She stroked his cheek a few times. He was back to the rolling eyes behind his closed lids, but he muttered something.

"Come on, Lex. It's almost dinner time. And you need a shower and fresh clothes."

He kicked and twitched a bit, but still didn't wake up.

Gina drew a long, slow breath through her nose. Lex was getting better. She was sure of it. And if Lex was getting better, then he could get up.

Gina started patting his cheek. Not too hard, but continually. At first he didn't respond. Then he made little complaining noises. She just kept at it until finally she heard her name. Weak, and quiet, but there.

"Gina?"

"Yes, honey." Gina's heart swelled with relief at hearing him speak. "I'm right here."

She leaned down and kissed his hot lips.

"I'm so tired, baby. Just let me sleep. Just a..."

"No, Lex." She grabbed the shoulders of his pajamas and grunted with effort as she hoisted him to a sitting position. "Honey, you need food. And you need a shower. So you need to wake up for a little bit. Then you can get some more sleep. I promise."

Lex sagged forward, half-asleep again already.

"Go 'way," he muttered. "Jus' go 'way..."

"I can't go away, honey. If you can't eat dinner, you're going to the hospital. It's been all I can do to keep you from getting dehydrated, the way you're sweating."

Took more patting/slapping to get Lex vertical, and she had to take most of his sopping weight to get him to the bathroom. So much for this blouse then. Another victim for the growing pile of laundry. And Gina wasn't even sure the washer and dryer were hooked up yet.

She had to manhandle Lex out of his wet things, and then she got him onto the folding lawn chair she'd put on the coral and seashell tiles of the shower stall. Those thin, pale green vinyl tubes wouldn't be the most comfortable things under his naked flesh, but a little discomfort would keep him awake.

Speaking of a little discomfort.

She turned on the taps. The pipes shook a bit, then started blasting water at Lex.

"Whuh?" he said, eyes snapping open, shifting about in the chair, arms tucked in tight for warmth.

"I'm sorry it's so cold, honey. But it'll warm up soon." She forced a bar of soap into his hand, jumping as the cold water hit her arm through the white blouse. "Scrub up, mister. That should help you wake up some too. You'll find your shampoo on the tiles in front of you when you're ready for it."

She watched until her shivering husband started rubbing the bar of soap under his arms. No doubt the poor dear could smell himself at this point, and that couldn't be helping him either.

Gina stuck one hand into the shower spray, relaxed a little when she felt the water warming up. She stepped back and pulled the curtain closed, then sighed and unbuttoned her blouse.

Tee shirts. Until Lex was past this, she'd have to stick to tee shirts. Then she wouldn't care if they got a little wet or sweaty. She stepped over to her open boxes of clothes, grabbed just such a shirt — teal, to go with her lime green slacks — and slipped it on.

She stripped the bed, and threw the sheets, comforter, and mattress pad into a laundry basket with Lex's pajamas and robe, and the shirts and bra she'd already had to abandon today. That was enough for one good load.

Out into the hall, then downstairs into the basement. The basement would make a great rumpus room, once they had a chance to really settle in. Despite the warm late afternoon above it, it managed to stay downright chilly. Must have been all the concrete — walls, floor and support pillars.

No doubt the family would practically live down here, come August. It was more than big enough for a good-sized game room and lounge. Practically the size of the whole first floor.

The washer and dryer were both set up and ready against one wall, with the box containing laundry soap, fabric softener, anti-cling dryer sheets and bleach sitting open on the smooth concrete floor in front of them.

God bless her Lex. When he'd found the time to do this, she didn't know.

She got the laundry started, then hustled back upstairs to check on her man. Lex was actually standing to wash his back. He looked better than he had since ... well, since before he got sick.

Gina smiled and went back to the kitchen to check on yesterday's lasagna. Normally she might have felt bad about serving the same meal two days in row, but with their bellies full of salt water taffy yesterday, her kids had hardly touched the lasagna last night.

Also, and it pained her to think it, Gina just hadn't had time to cook today.

The lasagna was just about ready, and she still had some of the last salad she'd made in Sunnyvale in a big Tupperware bowl.

Gina quick-stepped up the spiral, wrought-iron stairs to the second floor and started gathering the troops. Dee had still been sulking, but sulking with her sketch pad. Probably drawing Sebastian or something. Eli and Byron, for some reason, were in Byron's room looking at a book. Surprising, but probably good for both of them, even if Byron's room was still a state.

But all her children started finishing up what they were doing, with promises to be at the table in ten minutes.

Down the back stairs for Gina now — she mused that all these stairs had to be great exercise — to check on Lex.

He'd turned the water off, and sat hunched forward on the aluminum lawn chair. Dozing.

Gina sighed.

"Lex, honey?" She jostled his shoulder. "Lex?"

"Huh?" His head came up slow, and his eyes didn't open by a lot, but he did wake up. And right now, that was something. "Gina?"

"Come on, honey. Let's get you into your old pajamas so you can come eat dinner with your kids."

"No. Jus' ... wanna ... sleep." Lex sagged forward again.

"No," she said. "You'll sleep soon, I promise. But you *need* to eat."

Gina grabbed a fluffy white towel and started drying her husband. She probably could have been more gentle, but she had no intention of letting him sleep through this anyway. By the time she was done, Lex was on his feet, out of the shower stall, and leaning against the coral and seashell tiles of the divider between the shower and bathtub.

His breathing was slow and heavy, and his eyes were heavy-lidded, but he was standing — more or less — under his own power. And he was awake.

Gina fetched his old pajamas. They had started life as a pale blue, and they'd faded so much by now that they looked white in places, and were worn thin enough in spots that she could see his chest hair, if she tried.

But they fit, and they covered him enough for decency. They would do.

Gina helped him dress, then slipped under his shoulder, clutched him tight around the waist, and started helping her husband down the hall to dinner.

LEX WASN'T SURE WHERE HE WAS. NOT REALLY.

He knew he was having dinner with Gina and the kids. Which was good because he was hungry. Really hungry. They were all gathered around the dining room table in their normal spots. Lex at one end. Mason on his right and Eli on his left. Then Dee and Byron. Then Ava and Roy. Finally, Gina at the other end.

But this wasn't their condo. It was way too...

This was a house. A house full of hardwood. Cherry hardwood.

Wait. That was right. Lex had bought a house. And a job.

No. He hadn't bought a job. He'd *taken* a job. A big job. In some little Podunk town.

Cedars. Yes. He could smell cedar trees on the afternoon breeze. This was Cedar Street. Their new house on Cedar Street.

And this was definitely Gina's lasagna, chewy and cheesy and perfect. Perfect as the woman who made it. His Gina. His sweet Gina.

Weren't they fighting about something?

Lex had this conversation with himself several times over the course of dinner. He'd sip his water, and have a bite of his lasagna or his green salad with oil and vinegar dressing. He'd try to follow whatever conversation the kids and Gina were having.

But then...

Lex wasn't sure what then. It was foggy. Misty.

And when it got foggy ... or misty ... Lex wasn't where he was right now. Except that he kind of was. He was in this house, he thought. Only his stuff wasn't here. Someone else's was. And he wasn't alone. Except that he was. He was alone because Gina wasn't here. Or the kids. But he *wasn't* alone, because someone else *was* here. Big guy. Pale.

Couldn't get a good look at him though. Only sideways. Only from the edges of Lex's vision while he wandered room to room, looking for ... Gina? Was it Gina he was looking for?

Except that Lex wasn't wandering anywhere. And he wasn't wearing overalls either. He was wearing his old blue pajamas. And he was sitting...

He knew he was in a loop. He could never have said so aloud. Wouldn't have known how to say it. Where to begin. Nothing made sense, not even to him. That big, pale man. Lex had been dreaming about him. Hadn't he? He wasn't sure.

Wasn't sure what was a dream and what wasn't. Wasn't sure he wasn't asleep right now, dreaming of Gina's lasagna.

Except that when Lex dreamed of Gina, he didn't dream of lasagna.

On the other hand, he was hungry right now. So why not dream of lasagna? Or why not take another bite of the one in front of him. The kids were talking again, but their words weren't making any sense. Not even when they looked at Lex.

Must have been the fever. Yes. Lex remembered that he had a fever. And he *was* hot. Except that he was cold. Really cold. His forehead was hot. And under his collar. But his sides, even the back of his neck, and up his spine. All cold.

Hot and cold. At the same time.

Another sip of ... his water glass was empty now. And his plate was empty too.

Gina was next to him now. She had on that tight teal shirt. Lex smiled at the view.

She was saying something. Something happy sounding. Maybe Lex had eaten all his food? Yes. That must have been it. He didn't feel so hungry now.

Then Mason was beside him, and Eli. His boys. His big, strong boys. Helping Lex to his feet. Helping Lex down the hall. Into his room. Dee was beside his bed. Straightening the blankets. She was growing so pretty. Like her mother. Break hearts someday.

White sheets on the bed when Gina tucked him in. Why the white sheets? She hated them. Kept them only as backups.

Didn't matter...

Not really...

Lex was asleep the moment his head hit the pillow.

He started dreaming again.

The ditch dream came first.

Lex was in the backyard, with a great big spade in his hands. Bigger than it should have been. He was wearing the overalls for this dream. No shirt though, but he didn't need one. It would have just been one more thing sopping up his sweat. And his skin was so tanned he didn't need to worry about sunburn.

His back was sore from all the digging. And his arms and legs were sore. His hands were red and a little raw, blistering in places. But the ditch was only half-dug. Lex was standing in the waist-deep hole. It was more than long enough for him to lie down in, if he wanted to, but lying down would be a mistake.

Lying down led to beatings. And the beatings, once they started they didn't stop anytime soon.

So Lex kept digging. The dirt was hard and dark. He had to drive the tip of the shovel in, then stomp on it with his work boots just to manage a shovelful of dirt he could then send cascading over his right shoulder onto the grass. Onto the rough pile of dirt he'd been building steadily.

Shouldn't Lex have thrown the dirt over his *left* shoulder? Shouldn't he have been driving the shovel with his right hand? Not his left? Lex was right handed, and while he couldn't remember ever digging something this deep, he could remember how he dug. And this wasn't it.

But it was what he was doing, and he didn't want to stop. Stopping, that could lead to beatings too. But the voice would come first.

The deep mean voice. The voice that didn't care about blistered hands or sore muscles. Or dry, parched lips and tongue.

The voice wanted the hole dug, or the beatings would come again.

And so Lex dug. And dug. And dug.

Until the dream changed again.

He was inside now. Somewhere.

The room was cold, and dark. The floor was poured concrete. So were the walls. And the support pillars. Unpainted drywall for the ceiling. There was a light bulb hanging from the ceiling, but it wasn't lit.

Lex couldn't see a dangle chain, and he couldn't see a switch. In fact, he couldn't see far in any direction. Too dark.

Footsteps. Heavy. Thumping down concrete steps to Lex's right.

Lex was wearing pajamas, he realized. His good striped ones. And his tartan bathrobe too. No slippers though. Why would he be out like this in his pajamas and robe? Especially with no slippers?

Lex crouched. Looked toward the steps.

The light bulb flared to life. Yellow glare on the gray concrete. Lex had to blink against the brightness.

When his eyes adjusted, the man was standing in front of him. Big, angry red scar down the middle of his pale face. No. Pale didn't cover it. Ghost white. Sheet white. His skin was white like freezer frost. Bald head. Hairless chest, muscled like from a life of hard work and only recent lifting. His arms and pecks too big for his frame.

They fit his fingers, though. Those fat, scarred sausage fingers on hands like hams.

Hams. Lex could smell ham.

At least the guy was wearing pants. Faded jeans, torn at both knees — not the fashionable kind of fading and tearing, but jeans that had been worked half to death.

Something about this guy was familiar. Something about Gina. Or maybe a boxing match...

"Did I see you fight Mike Tyson?"

The guy didn't answer. He looked angry. Clenched jaw. Narrowed black eyes. Chest heaving with every breath. And the cold coming off of him. This guy was like a freezer with the door open, even in this cold basement...

Basement. This was the basement of Lex's new house. He didn't recognize it without the boxes, and the laundry units.

"This is my basement," Lex said. "You're not supposed to be here."

The man didn't budge.

"What's your deal?" said Lex. "This is private property and you're trespassing."

"Mine." The word came out smoother than Lex would have dreamed. He expected this guy to have a rough, whiskey voice. But it came out like tenor velvet. "Mine once. Mine always."

Lex remembered. Gina and her dream. The man in the shower.

This man scared Gina.

"All right, you son of a bitch," said Lex, wishing he was wearing something more formidable than pajamas and a bathrobe. "You get the hell out of my house, and you leave my family alone. And if you ever — *ever* — come near my wife again that scar will be the prettiest part of you left. You hear me?"

The man smiled, and that smile had nothing of humor to it. When Lex saw that smile, for the first time, he wondered if there might be some truth to the idea that some people are just plain evil.

Snake-quick the man grabbed Lex. Vise grip on his arms. Came in like to bite him.

Lex slammed his forehead into the man's nose. Felt it break. Felt a trickle of cold blood.

The man picked Lex up. Straight overhead. Threw him into a support pillar.

Lex once got hit by a baseball bat. He was playing high school ball at the time, didn't see the batter taking warm-up swings and the batter didn't see him. The aluminum bat caught Lex in the rib cage. Broke two and cracked another.

Slamming into the pillar felt exactly like that bat swing. Pain radiated out. Made him hiss for breath.

The man came closing in, weight low. Arms wide.

Lex pushed through the fiery pain in his back. Dove at the man's legs. Mason wasn't the first member of Lex's family to play football, and Lex knew how to tackle.

And Lex wasn't worried about drawing a flag.

Lex slammed his shoulder hard into the man's knees. Felt one pop.

The man never made a sound.

They came down together in a heap. Punching and kicking each other.

But the man got his hands on Lex. And the man had so much strength. Lex, Lex was feeling weak after that rush. Tired. Like he'd fought this fight before. Like maybe he'd always been fighting it. And the fatigue was wearing on him, even if it didn't seem to be wearing on the scarred man. The fatigue, and the pain from Lex's ribs, and the aches of a thousand punches from the scarred man.

So when the man got his hands on Lex, Lex couldn't stop the man from slamming him down onto the concrete. The man sat on Lex's broken ribs, spiking more hot pain. Every breath felt like it came across broken glass.

The man licked his smiling lips, a dark glint in his eyes.

Slammed Lex's head into the concrete.

Once.

Twice.

Three times.

Each one an explosion of fresh agony.

Lex was woozy. Barely hanging on. Fighting to hang on. But the room spun around him, and he wanted to throw up, and he was tired. So tired.

The man slammed Lex's head onto the concrete one more time.

And Lex blacked out.

INTERVIEW SNIPPET

Excerpt from 1996 interview with Barclay "Bones" McElroy

I knew you were going to ask me about that night. Told myself, they say they just want to ask a few questions, but you know what they really want to ask you. Once they work themselves up to it.

Not like you're the first people to ask.

So I'll tell you what I told the others.

I never got to talk to the man Lex too much, not before everything got going and definitely not after. We only really had that one conversation. That one where he was going to invite me over for dinner.

Such a good cook, he said his wife was. And the way he smiled when he said it, like the sun rose and set on that woman. Seemed like a good man. Much as I could tell from one conversation, anyway. And what little I saw during my vigil.

Did see the way he laughed and sang with his kids, the day he took them on that road trip.

Even so. Didn't have to be Lex's best friend to know that something had changed. Not after what happened that one night.

No, I'm not saying it had anything to do with the g-word. I answered your questions about the priest, but I'm not saying that anything Lex did was anything but his own doing.

I barely knew the man. No idea what he was capable of, nor any reason I should have known.

And don't you go putting words in my mouth. I know what the other neighbors have to say, but let me tell you, not one of them talked with Alexander Dumas, not any more than I did. And most of them, they didn't even exchange *that* many words.

No, I'm not sayin' the man did it all on his own. I'm not sayin' that either.

I don't know.

I just think ... I just think maybe that house is evil. And I know you and your crew are all dead set on spending the night there, but you couldn't pay me enough money to make me do it.

No. Not enough money in the world to make me spend the night in that house.

5

———

Thursday June 15th, 1989. Day Four

Midnight

Dee awoke to a silent house.

She lay huddled in her own bed, sheets and blanket tucked up under her chin. Her windows closed. The night air chilly, but not moving.

Her mouth was dry. Only the barest mint taste remained of her toothpaste, and her tongue almost swollen for want of saliva.

No footsteps in the attic. No scratching at the walls. No strange sounds. No sounds at all. Not even the wind in the trees outside, or the distant rumble of the nightly freight train. The bright moonlight came into her room unbroken by shadows.

The whole house seemed to be holding its breath. And Dee held hers along with it.

She glanced through her open door and across the hall.

Eli's door was closed.

Dee's stomach quivered. She drew a shaky breath. Alone. Something was wrong, and she was alone. The house was cold, and she was alone.

She needed Eli. And she was alone.

Dee closed her eyes, strained with her ears. She must have heard something. Something must have woken her. She'd been dreaming about...

She hadn't been dreaming at all. Not that she could remember. But Dee always remembered her dreams. Half of them ended up as drawings.

Something was wrong. Something was very wrong.

If Eli were with her, Dee might have been brave. Might have gone looking. Checked on Ava and Roy. Checked on Mason and Byron. Nothing *seemed* amiss. Only ... still.

But Dee did not have Eli. And the lack made her feel empty. Weak. Afraid.

Dee couldn't even brave the floor of her room to close her own door. To shut out the rest of the house. To feel just that little bit safer.

So Dee huddled into her blankets. And trembled.

Eli lay awake, staring at his closed white door, twilit at the edge of the bright moonlight.

Dee was just across the hall, on the other side of that door. And she was awake, too. Eli couldn't feel her right now, but was sure she was awake. If he was awake — and Eli didn't know why he was awake when he *had* been sleeping — then the odds were that Dee was awake too. That was how it worked. That was how it always worked.

But Eli wasn't sure how things were *supposed* to work.

Eli wasn't *supposed* to be so close with Dee. Mom said so. Mason said so. Dr. Clyburn said so. So Eli was doing the right thing, wasn't he? Closing his door? The one in his mind as well as the one across the room from him.

The door in his mind, that was something Dr. Clyburn had mentioned years ago. Eli'd forgotten all about it, until his long talk with Byron today. Byron. Who knew the little pipsqueak could be so smart about so many things?

Byron said that Eli and Dee had a "psychic connection." That they're minds were together even when their bodies were apart. Said it happened only once in maybe a hundred sets of twins. Maybe a thousand. No one knew for sure. But it was rare. Byron said it was a gift, and that was the first time anyone had ever said anything good about how close Eli and Dee were.

Byron read a lot, but that didn't mean he was right. Maybe. If it was so rare, maybe it wasn't a gift. Maybe it was a mistake.

How was Eli supposed to know?

And that "psychic connection" idea was only one of the things Byron had said today.

Byron talked about ghosts and hauntings and possessions and maybe demons. Eli wasn't sure. So many words and so many books. Byron had talked and talked and talked like he'd never had anyone to talk to before in his life.

And maybe he hadn't. Not about this stuff.

It was all too much. Eli couldn't keep it all in his head. He knew Byron thought Dad was fighting a ghost or something, and that we all had to pray that Dad won.

But of course Dad would win. Dad always won. Sales prizes, raffles — it was Dad's luck that Byron inherited with games and stuff. Dad always came up a winner.

Still, Byron insisted that Eli pray before bed tonight. And Eli meant to. He really did. But had he done it? Honestly, he couldn't remember. By the time Eli got ready for bed that night, he was exhausted. And not just from basketball, or schlepping Dad down the hall after dinner.

Closing that door in Eli's head, that hadn't been easy. Took effort. Tired him out. Tired him out enough that Eli fell asleep long before he expected to.

But he was awake now. And if the door in his head was closed, then it shouldn't have been Dee waking Eli up.

So why was Eli awake?

No footsteps from the attic. No scratching from the walls. Not even any water running through the pipes. Quiet house. Quieter than Eli had heard it since he set foot in the house on that first day.

But it was chilly. The evening had been warm when Eli got into bed. Even threw off his blanket. But he'd pulled it up in his sleep. Didn't Byron say that unnatural cold was a sign of ... of something. Was cold a ghost or a demon? Eli wasn't sure.

The air was still. That made sense, because the windows were closed. But that wasn't why. Eli could feel it. Or he thought he could. Byron's thousand ideas were all in Eli's head now, and he wasn't sure what he was thinking. What he was feeling.

He ... he felt alone. Maybe that was why the room felt so still. The house too.

Maybe closing that door in his head wasn't such a good idea after all.

Maybe Mom ... maybe Mason ... maybe they were wrong about this one.

Eli just didn't know.

So he huddled there in his bed and tried to figure it out.

Gina knew something was wrong the instant she woke up. But she needed a moment to realize what.

The house was quiet. The gibbous moon shone bright through the closed windows, illuminating all the boxes she and Lex had yet to unpack.

Lex. Where was Lex?

The bed beside her was empty but for the damp region where Lex had been tossing, turning and sweating for most of the evening. The covers on his side of the bed had been thrown off, either in his restless sleep or in haste to get up. She could still smell his oily-sick sweat.

The poor dear. Probably got up to pee and fell asleep again on the toilet.

Gina felt nearly that tired herself. She was tempted to shove her face back into her soft, soft pillow and go back to sleep. Wrangling the kids, unpacking, and trying to tend to Lex while keeping everyone calm about that sudden flu had just plain worn her out.

She hadn't even bothered putting on her nightgown before bed, and now she was regretting her haste. The night air was chilly, and everywhere the air touched it raised goose bumps. She pulled the covers tight to her chin.

"Lex," she stage whispered. "You in the bathroom, hon?"

Nothing.

Gina muttered the handful of curse words that were all she remembered of the Italian her mother forced on her. Could she let him sleep on the toilet? The thought had its appeal. He wouldn't be overheated by the covers. No risk of an accident occurring because he was too tired to get out of bed. A faucet was right next to him if he needed a drink. And her pillow was just *so very comfortable.*

Maybe she could let him nap there for a few minutes. If he was good enough to get up on his own to go to the bathroom, his fever had probably broken. He'd probably wake up in a few minutes and come back in. Probably be embarrassed to see that he'd woken Gina.

Yes, she told herself, nuzzling her sleepy head back into her soft white pillow. He would probably return ... any second ... now....

But what if he didn't?

Gina sat up, fully awake now.

What if Lex had stood over the toilet to pee and passed out? Hit his head on the tile?

Her husband could be lying unconscious on her bathroom floor right now.

So much for sleep.

Gina shivered naked in the cool air as she got up, and dug her red flannel, winter bathrobe out of a box, welcoming its warmth as she slipped into it and tied it tight. She couldn't find her slippers, and the hardwood floor was cold underfoot as she shuffled toward the bathroom.

She flipped on the light switch.

Lex wasn't on the toilet. The seat and the lid were down.

Gina crossed the cold, smooth tile — sparing a thought to remind herself that this house needed throw rugs — and lifted the lid. Pure clear water. Lex hadn't even peed and left without flushing to avoid waking her up, as he'd done for years.

She would have rather he flushed every time, but she could not break him of this habit.

He wasn't in the tub either. Maybe he'd gone into the kitchen for a snack, or...

The shower. Gina hadn't checked the shower.

Her belly quivered, her thighs pulled together, and a shiver ran up her spine. Gina didn't want to look in the shower.

That was silly. Father Andrew had blessed the whole house. He'd even blessed the shower stall after Gina told him the story. Told him what she'd seen in there. That ghost was gone. Gina'd even showered earlier herself in perfect ease and comfort.

Maybe it was the late hour. Maybe it was her missing husband. Gina wasn't sure why, but she didn't want to look in the shower now. The house ... the house didn't feel right. Didn't feel as safe as it had when Father Andrew was there.

But she was being silly. Gina knew that too. There was no reason she shouldn't look in that shower.

Gina closed her eyes. Puffed out a breath. Clenched her jaw and raised her fists. The shower stall would be empty. It had to be empty. There couldn't be a pale man with an angry red scar down his face. There just couldn't.

Gina opened her eyes. With a sigh of determination through her nose, she strode in front of the shower stall and looked inside, fists raised to defend herself.

The stall was empty, but for the aluminum lawn chair that remained after Lex's pre-dinner shower.

So where was Lex?

Gina flicked off the bathroom light and stood there in the doorway, giving her eyes a moment to adjust. He might have gotten hungry. Much energy as the poor dear had used up fighting that nasty flu. That made sense. He had to be in the kitchen, making one of his famous peanut butter and banana sandwiches on whole wheat.

She would check there next.

Gina started through the bedroom, but stopped dead halfway across when she spotted movement through the bedroom window.

Someone was in their backyard.

Gina's heart all but stopped. An intruder? She stepped into the shadows. Trying not to make a sound. Trying not to even breathe. Slipped up beside the windowsill. Ducked down and angled to peek without being seen.

Someone was digging a hole in her backyard. Someone facing away from her. Bent forward.

Who would...

But then Gina's eyes focused on the sight of faded, threadbare pajamas.

Lex?

⁂

DIGGING. DIGGING WAS WHAT MATTERED. LEX KNEW. HE'D DREAMED this dream before. Dreamed it forever, felt like.

The dream didn't always start the same. Usually it started with the digging. But not always. It could start with him wandering through the house, or even having dinner. Or doing his homework. Then he'd have to fetch the shovel to start digging. Like this time.

Sometimes it ended with the digging. When Lex was smart. When Lex was a good boy. When Lex did what he was supposed to. Then he could dig and dig until the dream changed.

In that way, the digging was a break. Much better than the fighting. And even the fighting was better than the other dreams.

But Lex didn't need to think about the other dreams. Not now. This was the digging dream, so Lex had to dig.

Lex knew what he had to do the moment the dream shifted and he opened his eyes. He'd been in bed with Gina then. In bed with naked Gina, but it wasn't that kind of dream. It was the digging dream. He'd felt it in his bones. Felt it in his hands.

And when Lex had that feeling, he needed to get to the shovel. A.S.A.P. Any delays might lead to the voice. To the beatings.

So Lex had hustled barefoot across the hardwood floor and into the white tile mudroom behind the stairs, and from there to the back door and out into the chilly night air. The moon above was almost full. That was good. Sometimes he had to dig under the dark moon, and then the voice was always in a bad mood.

He shivered in his old, faded blue pajamas, but cold was no excuse for not digging. The activity would warm him soon enough.

The grass was soft under his feet as Lex trotted all the way across the back lawn toward that one spot along the redwood fence. Not over by the orange, almond, or lemon trees toward that one corner, or by the monkey bars and swing set in the middle of the yard, but back at the back, past the row of purple begonias. That was where he'd find the old shovel. Behind the extra-thick cedar tree, it waited. Rough handle and rusty blade, leaning there against the tree. That was where he always found the shovel, and even in this weird version of the dream — a version where he could smell cedar and grass and begonias and not nearly as much ham as usual — even here the shovel was waiting.

So Lex had grabbed the rough handle in his hand and started trotting back across the grass. Wishing again, like he did every time, that this time he'd get a pair of gloves and save his hands.

But no gloves this time either. This time he didn't even get the work boots or the overalls.

Lex reached the digging spot — twelve paces straight out from the back door, a good ten yards from the nearest fence on the east side. This was the hidden spot. Where the cedars lining the sides of the house hid Lex and his digging from the prying eyes of neighbors.

Good boys didn't dig where anyone could see. Digging was a punishment. A private thing. Lex had been bad. Defiant. Said no and no and no so many times he could barely remember what he'd been saying no to.

Didn't matter now. Lex had been bad, and bad boys had to dig if they knew what was good for them. And if they didn't, then they got worse than digging.

So Lex had started to dig.

The ground was soft this time. That was different. Most times, the ground was hard under the spade and Lex had to stomp on it with his boot to get it to cut the earth. But this ground was softer, as from a recent rain.

Lex had dug out the whole shape without once touching his foot to the blade. Now he had a rectangle some six feet long and four feet wide. That was the right shape. It just needed to get deeper. A lot deeper.

Lex was maybe ankle deep when the ground got tougher. Lex's hands were red and raw now, with maybe a dozen little slivers scattered around from the rough wooden handle.

Splinters were no excuse. Lex needed to dig.

But the ground was too tough to just ram the shovel in now. He started having to put his heel to the rusty blade to split the earth.

Soon Lex was almost knee-deep. His foot hurt. His hands hurt. His arms and back were sore and stiff. But Lex was making headway, like a good boy. Before long the dream would shift. Maybe this time he'd even get a reward.

Didn't good boys deserve a reward?

"Lex?"

Gina's voice? What was Gina doing here? Gina was never in the digging dream.

But she was this time. She was standing there at the edge of the hole, barefoot and shaking in her red flannel bathrobe.

"Lex, honey, what are you *doing?*"

Lex blinked at her. Looked at the hole. Looked back at her. Kicked the shovel into the earth for more dirt.

"Honey, stop!" Her hands on his shoulders now. Shaking him. "You're bleeding! Oh, Lex. Your hands. Your foot. Come out of there."

Lex turned back for another shovelful of dirt.

Gina's voice got sharp.

"Lex! You stop digging this instant and come out of there."

"I have to dig," he said, as though this were the most obvious thing in the world. Which it was, really. Why didn't she get that? "Bad boys have to dig."

"What are you talking about? Come out of there."

"No! I have to dig. Or the beatings start!"

He forced up another shovelful of dirt, tossed it over his right shoulder toward the growing pile of earth.

Gina grabbed the shovel near the blade.

"Ow! This thing's all splintery, Lex. Where'd you get it?"

But she held on. Tried to pull it away.

Lex gripped harder with his painful, bleeding hands.

"No!" He yanked it back away from her. "I have to dig."

He turned back to his hole.

"Fine," he heard her say, and she had resigned exasperation in her voice. Good. Maybe she'd...

But she wasn't done talking.

"I'll get the boys. And maybe Bones. And maybe Father Andrew. Don't worry, honey. We'll get you the help you need."

Lex's boys. His big strong boys. And that Bones, he was a big man too. And a priest? Gina wanted to bring her priest back here? Now?

She wasn't going to let him dig. She wasn't going to let Lex be a good boy.

That was bad.

Lex turned back to her.

"No digging?" he said. He had to be sure she meant it. Because she couldn't mean it. She just couldn't. Gina was a good girl, wasn't she?

"No digging." Gina had her hands on her hips and that no-nonsense tone to her voice. No way to argue with her when she was like this.

"No digging then," said Lex with a sigh. He raised the shovel. "I guess it has to be beatings."

GINA SCREAMED.

That look in Lex's eye. Rage. Murder. Not like her husband at all, standing there in his worn pajamas. In the hole he'd been digging in their backyard.

She'd only ever seen that look once before.

In the hateful black eyes of the pale, scarred man.

Lex held the shovel high and leaped out of the hole. Rictus smile on his face in the bright moonlight. Landed on bloody feet next to her. He smelled like sweat and dirt — and ham?

Gina turned. Ran for the back door.

The shovel slammed into her back. Right by the spine.

Air *whuffed* out of her. Dull pain roiled through her torso, out from a sharp center. Gina fell. More pain from her ribs, throbbing with each rapid heartbeat. Soft grass filled her mouth. Tears flooded her eyes.

Gina scrambled forward on all fours. Spared a look back.

Lex stood there, confused, just outside his hole. Holding a broken shovel in bloody hands.

"Gina?" he said.

But Gina didn't wait. She scrabbled up the three concrete steps and through the door. Slammed it behind her. Twisted the handle lock. Yanked the chain into place.

Then fell against the door, her world full of pain and tears.

WHATEVER HAD WOKEN DEE SEEMED TO HAVE PASSED. SHE HADN'T heard any noises. Hadn't seen or even felt anything that might have jarred her out of sleep. And she couldn't feel Eli, so she didn't think it could have been something Eli was reacting to.

So Dee was just settling back into bed to try to sleep when her mother screamed.

Dee froze. She couldn't think.

That couldn't have been Mom. But...

Dee threw off the blankets. Her heart was pounding. She could feel it in her throat. Hear the blood rushing past her ears. Her breaths came fast and shallow. The air was cold. So cold in her baby blue nightgown. But there was no time to change.

A door slammed.

Mom. Mom was in trouble.

Dee got to the hall at the same time doors started flinging open all around her. Suddenly Eli in his purple pajama bottoms was in the hall with her, close enough to touch but too distant to feel. Face tense, like he heard the scream.

Mason didn't pause. He had on jeans and a Giants tee-shirt, but no socks or shoes, and he was already bounding down the back stairs three at a time.

Eli looked at Dee, confused. Like the distance between them hurt him too and he didn't know what to say. What to do.

"Help Mason," she said. "I'll gather the troops."

Eli nodded, shaky and goose bumped, and started for the back stairs.

Dee looked up and down the hall. Arms in tight. So cold. But no time for that.

She started with Byron's door. Knocked.

"Byron? It's Dee." She tried the handle, but it was locked. "Byron?"

"If you're really Dee, go back to your room."

"What do you mean—"

"*Go away!* No one's invited in here. Not into *my* room."

Dee didn't have time for this. He seemed to be all right. Back down the hall to the snotmonsters' rooms. Roy's door was open, and so was Ava's. Dee stood in the center of the hallway between them.

"Guys?" she called. "Roy? Ava? Come here, guys. It's cold tonight. Why don't we all go sleep in my bed?"

Ava peeked out from around her doorframe. She was in her astro-naut pajamas, but she held her hobby horse upside down so she could swing the stick part like a baseball bat.

"What was that scream?" she said. "Is Mom all right?"

"Mom's..." No. She wouldn't lie to them. "Mason and Eli are checking on Mom right now."

"Is it Daddy?" That was Roy's voice, and when Dee looked she could just see his eyes peeking out from under his bed.

"I don't know, guys. But Mason and Eli, they're big boys too. And they're down there helping Mom right now." Neither Roy nor Ava looked like they intended to budge from their hiding spots.

"Come on, guys," she said. "It's cold, and I'm not as brave as you two. Why don't you come snuggle in with me? Then we'll all be warm, and I'll feel safe, and when Mom comes to tell us everything's all right, we'll already be together. She can tell us all at once."

"Don't be scared, Dee," said Ava, coming out with her hobby horse held high. "I'll protect you."

"Me too," said Roy, not to be outdone. He came out in his cowboy pajamas and holding his silver-gray six-shooter popgun like it was a real pistol. "I'll keep you safe too."

"I'm already keeping her safe," said Ava. "You can't shoot anything with that—"

"I feel much safer already," said Dee, speaking over Ava and taking both their hands. "Come on, guys. Let's go."

Dee led them back to her room and closed and locked the door. She didn't like leaving Byron alone, but she couldn't make him open his door, and if she tried she'd just make everybody even more scared.

She wished she knew what was going on. But short of that, all she could do was keep the little ones safe. So she settled the three of them into her bed, Ava on her right and Roy on her left.

She wished she had a phone. Her room had a plug for it, but Mom said their phone company appointment wasn't until next week. If things got bad, maybe she could sneak downstairs to the kitchen phone. Or maybe she'd sneak out onto the roof and look for help.

She wished she could feel Eli. He picked the worst time possible to cut himself off from her.

Dee snuggled down into the covers, while Ava and Roy fidgeted around her. Dee stared at the ceiling, and waited.

Eli got down the wide, back stairs and wasn't sure which way to go down the hall. Mom and Dad's room? The front? The house seemed qui—

"Slow down, Mom. You're not making sense."

Mason's voice. Coming from the mud room. No more than a dozen steps away.

The mud room was the only room in the house that didn't have a hardwood floor. The floor was white tile, like a bathroom, and it had two drains: one in the center and one off to the side. The walls were tile too, two-thirds the way up, before they gave way to more cherry hardwood. Near the side drain was a hose and a faucet.

Mom was leaning against the back door, in the middle of the back wall. She looked scared. Wide-eyed, same scared look Dee had. But Mom had tears on her face too. And she was breathing fast and shallow. Her red flannel robe was grass-stained.

Mason stood over her, hands on her shoulders.

"Where's Dad?" said Eli, still standing in the doorway. Not sure if he should come in or not. "What's going on?"

"Go back to bed," said Mason. "I got this."

Mom reached up and lifted Mason's hands off her shoulders. She started to draw a deep breath, but winced and made a small sound.

"Eli," said Mom through gritted teeth, "your brother isn't listening to me."

"Gina?" Dad's voice, from the other side of the back door, accompanied by a soft knock. "What's going on? Let me in."

Mason reached for the safety chain and Mom slapped his hand.

Mason pulled his hand back like she'd slapped his face.

"Not just yet, honey," she called loudly through the door, cringing like talking hurt. "Don't worry, though. We'll get you back in here soon."

Eli's jaw dropped. Mason was right. This wasn't making any sense at all.

"Eli," said Mom, again through clenched teeth, "I want you to go across the street and fetch Mr. McElroy. Tell him to bring whatever he can. Antiseptic. Bandages. And Mason," — she held up an admonishing finger, which meant it was getting serious — "I want you to go to the kitchen and call Father Andrew. His number's on the fridge."

"But, Mom—" started Mason, but Mom talked right over him.

"*Now*, Mason. Tell Father Andrew it's an emergency. He'll understand. Then bring me back some ibuprofen and a glass of water."

Maybe Father Andrew would understand but Eli sure didn't.

"Mom," he started, but he trailed off as he heard his father's voice.

"Gina, please. I know I was sleep-digging ... or something ... but I'm awake now, and I'm cold. And bleeding. My hands. My feet."

"Mom," said Mason, "I love you. But I am not going to let you keep my *sick father locked outside in the cold.*"

Too much. Too much was happening and Eli didn't understand any of it. Why was Dad outside? Why was Mom's robe grass-stained? What was that scream?

Wait. If Mom wanted a priest, then this maybe had something to do with that occult stuff Byron was going on about all afternoon.

If that was true, then Eli wasn't up to facing it alone.

Mason picked Mom up. Just picked her up like a doll. Eli's eyes got so wide the room got brighter.

Mom winced hard and hissed like it hurt, but Mason set her down against a side wall, out of the way.

"No, Mason," she said, but it came out weak. "Don't—"

Was Mom right? Or Mason? Eli didn't know what to do. Didn't know who to help. He couldn't do this. Not alone. He needed Dee. He needed Dee like he'd never needed her before. Only together — only through that psychic connection Bryon talked about — could they face whatever was going on. Eli needed his connection back. He needed it back now.

Mason threw open the locks.

Eli focused on that door in his head. The one that locked out Dee. And he threw it open as hard as he could. He threw it open wider than it had ever been before. Just as wide open as he could possibly make it.

Mason opened the back door.

And something came inside.

Dee sat bolt upright.

Roy and Ava tumbled aside, protesting. Both still wide awake.

Eli. Dee felt Eli. She was sure of it. Felt his fear, his worry. Something about Mom, and Dad, and Mason. And Mr. McElroy? And a priest?

Too many images hit her fast and hard. Nothing made sense.

And all of it just a flash of information. One single flash.

And then it was gone. Just as fast.

But the "gone" was different this time. It didn't feel like Eli cut himself off again. If felt more like ... like...

...like some*thing* swatted him away. Frozen terror washed over Dee.

Roy and Ava were bouncing and arguing, wound up and sleepy all at the same time.

But Dee couldn't spare any attention to quiet them.

Eli. What—

A scream pierced through the house.

Not Mom. Not Eli. Not any voice Dee ever heard before.

Roy and Ava clung to Dee. And she clung right back.

Gina couldn't remember the last time anything hurt as bad as her back.

Childbirth. Childbirth had to have been worse than this. But she couldn't remember that pain, exactly, and the burning through her back was fresh and all-too-present right now as she slumped against the white tile wall of the mudroom.

She still had tears in her eyes, but she didn't think they were all from the pain. Or even the humiliation of her own son literally setting her aside.

Lex stood framed by moonlight at the open back door. His worn blue pajamas sweat-stained and smelly. No rage in his eyes now. He looked as confused about all this as she felt.

But he had hit her. Her beloved Lex had hit her with a shovel. That was why every breath hurt. Why even sitting here against the tile hurt.

Or maybe it wasn't her Lex. Maybe it was the scarred man *acting* through Lex. The eyes. Lex's eyes had looked just like the scarred man's, the way he held that shovel. The way he leapt at her.

But now his eyes looked like Lex again. But Gina just wasn't sure.

It didn't help that Lex still had that old, splintery shovel handle in his red and raw hands.

Mason slipped under Lex's arm. Started helping him to the dog wash against the other side of mudroom. Lex dropped the shovel handle to clatter on the tiles.

Mason. Her eldest son. Her darling boy. He'd defied her. Let Lex back in. And who knows what came—

A scream. So loud it buzzed in her ears. Gina slapped her hands to the sides of her head. Hunched forward, hissing as more pain flared from her ribs. Through scrunched eyes she couldn't see who was screaming.

Lex and Mason looked down the hall. Past Eli.

Eli ... Eli just stood there, staring out the door into the moonlight. Eyes wide. Mouth hanging open. But he wasn't screaming. The scream came from somewhere behind him.

The scream finally ended. Gina's ears still roared in protest, dulled by the decibels of the assault.

Mason leaned Lex against the tile. Turned to investigate. Started for the hall.

Eli grinned.

The grin was awful. Wild. Not like anything Gina had ever seen on her sweet boy's face before. His whole face looked wrong now. The way he held his eyes, his neck, his cheeks. Not like...

Not like Eli at all.

Eli grabbed the broken shovel handle from the tiles. Turned after his brother.

"Eli, what are you—" started Lex.

"*Mason!*" Gina yelled. "*Look out!*"

Mason turned in time for Eli to stab his brother in the chest with the broken end of the shovel handle. The jagged point snapped. Mason fell backward to the hardwood of the hallway, head tucked forward. Arms slapping the wood like when he did judo. Blood on his orange Giants shirt. A pencil-sized sliver of wood sticking out of his chest.

Mason clutched at the wood. Cried out through clenched teeth as he yanked it out. More blood spreading on his shirt now.

Gina scrambled for her feet. Slow. Too slow. Pain like thunder from her neck to her hips.

Lex shook his head, fists at his temples. "No, no, no, no, no. No, no, no." Over and over.

Eli dove at Mason.

"I won't I won't I won't," said Lex.

Eli grabbed Mason around the throat. Started choking him. Blood flecked Mason's lips as he struggled for air. Mason slapped at Eli, nothing behind the blows.

"*Nonononononono,*" said Lex.

Gina screamed and threw herself at Eli.

She screamed again when she slammed into him. Her shoulder drove into his side. Her definitely broken ribs shifted. Spread pain like lava from her scalp to her toes.

But she broke his grip.

"*Byron, goddamn it!*" yelled Dee as she continued pounding on his door. "*Open this door right now.*"

The door finally opened a crack.

Dee shoved it wide open. Byron's eyes went wider than that. His mouth was working but he wasn't saying anything.

Good. Dee didn't need the interruption.

"Roy and Ava are in my room. Crying. You bring them in here and calm them down. I need to get downstairs."

Byron's eyes screwed up like *he* might start crying. Dee didn't have time for that.

She slapped him hard. Once.

"Pull it together, Byron. There's trouble and I need to help."

"But a ghost. And Dad. And—"

"*Now!*" Dee raised her hand again, but Byron held up his hands in surrender.

"Go then. But you're running into trouble."

Dee started to turn away, then turned back, suspicion all through her. "Do you know how to stop this ... whatever's happening?"

"No. You need like a priest or a Voodoo man or—"

Priest. Something about a priest had flashed through Dee's mind during her momentary reconnection with Eli.

"There's a number on the fridge. Call it. Get a priest and don't take no for an answer."

"What about—"

"*Now, Byron.*"

Byron hoofed it for the front stairs. Dee ducked her head back into her room. Stared at the crying Ava and Roy and couldn't think of a single thing to say to them. So she forced a smile that didn't fool anyone, then locked them in her room.

Dee turned and ran for the back stairs.

Pain narrowed Gina's vision. She saw the world through a hazy tunnel of red. And that tunnel was closing, slowly.

She was on top of Mason. Wheezing Mason. Mason sticky with blood. Blood on his chest. Bloody foam on his lips. More blood trickling out his chest. Mason whimpering under her weight.

Somewhere behind her Lex kept up his litany of refusal. Useless to her right now.

Didn't matter. Right now Eli was the problem.

Eli lay where the cherry hardwood wall met the cherry hardwood floor. Moaning. Holding the back of his head, where it slammed into the wall. His eyes were closed. Gina wasn't sure what she'd see when those eyes opened.

Wasn't sure she could risk finding out.

"Stay back," she said.

Eli moaned. Mason wheezed. Gina gritted her teeth against the pain, hissing each breath in and out.

Suddenly Dee was there. Bless the girl.

"Dee." Gina's voice was weak. She had to hope Dee could hear over her father's chanting. "Fridge. Number. Priest."

"Byron's on it," said Dee, kneeling beside Eli.

"No," said Gina, tears leaking out her eyes as she forced herself to a kneeling position, one hand instinctively holding closed her robe. "Don't."

Dee ignored her. Dee always ignored her when it came to Eli.

"Eli," said Dee. His eyes didn't open. But Dee kept talking. Fast and low, and whatever she was saying wasn't English. That damned twinspeak of theirs. This wasn't the time for...

"...was it?"

Eli wasn't doing anything but listening to her. His hands, though. His hands flexed and opened. Flexed and opened. But he listened.

Behind her Lex kept refusing. Kept denying it was happening, as though he could make it all go away with his words.

Gina sighed, and even that hurt. But she had no more time for her own pain. Not with her eldest boy still bleeding. She put her hands over the blood trickling out of Mason's chest, girded herself for the flare of pain that would come, and put pressure on the wound.

Mason whimpered. Tossed. His movements were so weak. That wasn't good. And the blood on his lips with every breath. And the bruises already forming on his neck. He needed an ambulance. A hospital.

Or at least Bones.

"Bones," she said aloud. But no one was listening.

"Lex," Gina said, though it came out as little more than a whisper. She drew a deep, painful breath, and screamed, *"Lex! Snap out of it! We need you!"*

The litany behind her stopped. The twinspeak beside her stopped.

Eli blinked his eyes open, and he looked like Eli. He said something to Dee in that private language of theirs.

"Eli's okay now," said Dee. "It's gone from him."

Did Dee know? Know about the ghost? Know what was happening?

Didn't matter. Not now.

"Get across the street, baby," said Gina. "Get Bones. We need him. Now."

Dee turned. But before she could take a step the back door slammed shut.

Then the door to Gina's and Lex's bedroom. More doors kept slamming. Every door in the house, from the sound of it. One by one by one.

Dee looked back, and Gina saw the fear in her eyes. The same fear Gina felt right now.

"There's a priest coming!" That was Byron's voice. From somewhere down the hall. The kitchen? "So you better move on, ghost. If you know what's good for you."

Father Andrew. Father Andrew was coming. Thank God. If the Heavenly Father would only get her family through this crisis, Gina'd personally see to it that her family went to church every Sunday for the rest of their lives.

"Good." That sounded like Lex's voice, but it was wrong. Wrong tone, wrong accent even. That one word sounded like Dakota or something.

Gina risked looking back over her shoulder.

Lex stood only two steps away. Holding the broken shovel handle.

Dark malevolence gleamed in his eyes. In his horrible smile. And the sick joy in his voice.

"Always wanted to off a priest."

<hr>

ELI UNDERSTOOD NOW. AND HE WISHED TO HEAVEN HE DIDN'T.

Eli'd thrown the door in his head too wide open, and that ghost — that foul scarred man who called himself Clay — waltzed right into Eli's head and took over. But Dee, she'd all but shared a brain with Eli his whole life. When Mom bought that moment by knocking Eli into the wall, Dee did the rest.

Eli was himself again. But Dad, standing there with the splintery broken shovel handle in his hand, Dad wasn't himself at all.

Dad raised the shovel handle.

"You're all bad." The words sounded smooth, but odd. Inflected wrong for Dad. "Beatings all around."

"You," said Mom, turning to face Dad. She sounded like every word hurt. "You leave my babies alone."

Dad grinned.

Mom leaped. Her fingers arched like claws.

Dad slammed the shovel handle into her ribs. Knocked her aside. Mom hit the tile in the mudroom and crumpled.

The shovel handle snapped with the blow. Even shorter now. But Dad — not Dad, *Clay* — Clay smiled.

"Come on, Eli," said Dee, tugging at his hand.

"No," said Eli, standing up. "You go get Bones. We need him."

"But—"

"Go!" And Eli could hear her feet slapping down the hall as she ran.

"All grown up, are you?" said Clay.

"I kicked you out of my head. Maybe I can kick you out of my dad."

Clay took a step closer. He was in the doorway of the mudroom now. Good. Eli could hear Mom's ragged breathing, and as long as blood kept coming from Mason's chest, at least that meant he was still alive.

But Eli needed to make sure Mom and Mason stayed alive.

"Come on, *Clayton*," said Eli as he backed away a few steps toward the basement stairs. A scowl told Eli he was right. Clay did hate his full name. "Not man enough to face a sixteen-year-old boy?"

Clay came forward all right. But as he did he rammed the end of the broken shovel handle into Mason's unprotected throat. Mason gurgled through gruesome snapping sounds. Then he stopped moving.

Mason. Mason couldn't be... Not dead. Not Mason.

Clay grinned with Dad's face and said, "You can't fool me boy. And for trying, it's double-punishment for you."

Tears in his eyes, Eli turned and ran for the basement. But he had no idea what he'd do when he got there.

———

THE FRONT DOOR WOULDN'T OPEN. WHY WOULDN'T IT OPEN?

Dee checked the locks again. The deadbolt was back. The handle lock was in the open position. And the security chain was dangling from its hook.

But the door wouldn't open.

Dee yanked and yanked at the handle.

"It's the ghost," said Byron, and Dee all but jumped out of her skin. What was he doing behind her? She spun around to make sure it was him and gave herself a second to catch her breath.

But only a second.

"Get to your room and lock the door," she said, turning back to the front door. "Dad's—"

"Possessed. I know. Father Andrew's coming."

"Hope he drives fast," said Dee, yanking on the door again.

"Windows won't open either," said Bryon. "I already tried."

"Fine." Dee strode past Byron to the dining room, while Byron trailed her, watching.

"Get back to your room," she told him. "And lock the door."

Dee didn't wait to see if he obeyed. She hefted one of the dining room chairs, then dropped it when a wave of fear and sadness washed over her. Eli. That was Eli.

"Mason's dead," she said, voice tiny with disbelief.

She heard Byron turn and bong up the wrought iron spiral staircase.

Good. He'd be safe at least. For a while. But Dee still needed help.

She hefted the chair again and threw it through the living room window. The crash was loud, but nothing compared to all the screaming earlier. Dee's ears still hurt from that.

A light turned on across the street. Bones' living room. She could see him getting up out of an armchair, red plaid shirt and ancient blue jeans.

"Mr. McElroy!" she yelled. "We need you! Please!"

Bones took a step forward, then stopped. He looked down. Was he biting his lip?

"Please! Bones!"

The old man's head came up again and he started moving.

Good. Now Dee could go help Eli. She turned and ran back down the hall.

THE BASEMENT WAS EVEN COLDER THAN THE UPSTAIRS. IT WAS ALL poured concrete — walls, floor and support pillars — and so cold that Eli's feet expected to slip on ice. The yellow light of the single dangling bulb threw shadows that seemed to move every time Eli turned his head.

Such a big place for one light bulb. Even a bright one like this.

But worse than the cold was the smell. Like blood and ham, strong enough that Eli's stomach wanted to turn.

And his stomach was already quivering. Mason. Dad had killed Mason.

No. Not Dad. Clay. Clay killed Mason. He just ... he just used

Dad's hands to do it.

And Eli had to figure out how to stop him. Or at least hold him off until help could…

Footstep on the stairs.

"The rules are simple." Dad's voice, but not Dad's words. "Disobedient boys dig. But bad boys, oh, bad boys need a beating."

Clay stood at the foot of the stairs now. Only about half an old shovel handle left, but it looked more than dangerous enough in the yellow light.

"And you've been a very, very bad boy."

Eli's head whipped around. There had to be something…

The laundry machines.

Eli ran for the laundry machines as Clay walked slowly closer on Dad's feet.

"Dad," said Eli, digging through the box in front of the washer. Hoping he'd find what he needed. "I know you're in there. Fight him, Dad. I know you can."

"Your dad," said Clay, shaking the jagged end of the shovel handle at Eli, "your dad was a very bad boy. Fought me all day and night, he did. But he can't fight me anymore."

"I did." Eli hefted the half-full jug of bleach.

"And now you'll be punished for it."

Clay came at him, shovel handle poised to swing, not stab.

Eli ripped the cap off the jug of bleach. Splashed high.

Clay screamed, but it sounded like anger and frustration. Not pain. Got his eyes closed in time. Maybe burning in his nose or mouth, but not enough. Not nearly enough.

Clay swung the shovel and knocked the jug out of Eli's hands.

Eli scampered over behind a support pillar.

"You're only making it worse for yourself," said Clay, swinging the shovel handle around and walking slowly closer. "I enjoy a good chase, myself."

"Come on then." Eli ran to another support pillar. There were six in all. Maybe he could keep this up until—

"You think help's coming." Clay started laughing. "Nobody can come into *my* house, boy. Just like no one can leave it. Not now that I'm here." Clay tapped Dad's chest. "No. In here I've got all the time I want."

Clay grinned.

"Time enough to kill each one of you, just as slow as I like."

DEE SHIVERED AS SHE SNUCK DOWN THE BASEMENT STAIRS. SO COLD. SO cold she could see her breath. And her in just this stupid nightgown.

She had Mom's tenderizer mallet from the kitchen in her right hand. She'd almost grabbed the butcher's knife, but she couldn't scare a ghost. She needed to knock out her dad. That was the only way she could think of to end this.

Dad was over there now. No. Not Dad. Yes. Not Dad was swinging that shovel handle, but not like he was serious. Eli was ducking behind support pillars, and Not Dad was mocking him. Calling him slow. Lazy. Stupid. And most of all, bad.

Eli knew she was here. She could feel him, clearer than she'd ever felt Eli before. She knew what Eli'd tried to do with the bleach, and she was sure he knew about the tenderizer.

Not Dad turned and looked at her. He grinned.

"Well," he said. "If it isn't the only good girl in the whole house. Come down here, good girl. Clay has a treat for you."

"Let me guess," Dee said, reaching the concrete floor now. "My treat is getting stabbed with a shovel handle?"

"Never!" Not Dad sounded downright offended, while Eli eased out from behind his pillar. Poised to spring. Not Dad continued, "Only bad girls get punished. Good girls get—"

Eli sprang at Not Dad, but Not Dad was ready. Spun in place, thrusting the broken shovel handle like a spear. Caught Eli in the shoulder. Stopped him in mid-air and dropped him to the concrete. The shovel handle jutted out of Eli's shoulder while he blinked and gasped.

Pain. So much pain. Dee could feel only the ghost of it, and it still radiated up to her neck and down across her stomach.

"Now, as I was saying," said Not Dad, stepping over to grab the shovel handle and finish the job.

Dee almost charged him. Almost raised the tenderizer mallet and ran screaming and swinging.

But she could feel Eli in her head. A cloud of pain, yes, but an idea.

Eli was on one side of Not Dad. Dee was on the other. And Dee understood.

Dee was already in touch with Eli's mind, but she reached anyway. She reached for him the way she had upstairs. Muttering all the while in their private language. Riffling through all their little shared jokes, shared pains, everything she could think of. Every moment from their lives that reflected how close she and Eli were.

And Eli, Eli was reaching for her the same way. Past his own pain, and muttering his own memories as he reached.

Together. They connected together tighter in that moment than they ever had before. Tighter than they'd been since the cells split that first separated them into two people instead of one.

This was a level of pure psychic synchronicity. They were two bodies, but one mind. One soul. Everything they had ever done, everything they had ever known, even the few things they had held back from each other, all shared now. All accepted now.

Two people, but one person.

And Clay — and Dee now knew that Not Dad's name was Clay just as she knew it was short for Clayton — that dead man, was stuck between them. But in the space between Eli and Dee — the physical space, the emotional space, and the psychic space — there was no room for something like Clay.

Dad was a complete individual. Mind, body and soul. The connection between Eli and Dee posed no threat to him.

But Clay, he was a broken soul and a broken mind without a body of his own. When that perfect connection forged between Eli and Dee, it left no room for something like Clay.

Clay was evicted from Dad. And there was nowhere close to go.

INTERVIEW SNIPPET

Excerpt from 1996 interview with Barclay "Bones" McElroy

Look. It happened just like I told you, and this is the last time I'm tellin' it.

Yeah, I almost let fear get the better of me. If you'd spent as long as I have listening to folks talk about how haunted that house was... If you'd heard the screams I'd heard that night, well, maybe you would have been scared to go over there too.

Yeah, you just look at me that way. Got half a mind to walk out of here right now. But someone else will just ask the same damn questions, so I might as well go through it on camera.

One. More. Time.

When that little girl yelled for me a second time, well, I found my shame and I got my feet moving. I still keep an old field pack near the door. Fresh supplies in it of course. I threw on my shoes, grabbed that pack, and hot-footed it across the street.

I couldn't get that front door open. And I must have tried a dozen times. The handle turned right, but no good. So I figured there had to be something blocking it. I tried to get in through that broken window instead.

Must have been some sight. Old man like me trying to climb in through an open window. Damnedest thing though. I couldn't get a grip on the windowsill to haul myself up. Got pretty desperate. Don't know how long I tried to do it.

I do know that I was hearing more crashing and yelling and screaming coming from the house. And I felt like a damned fool that I didn't call the cops before coming over, but I couldn't take the time to go back and do it then. I had to get inside.

Then that young priest came pulling up in that stupid little Japanese car of his. And *he* wants to try the door, but he doesn't have any better luck than I do.

Maybe he was a little smarter than me, though. Because he took one look at that window and said, "Let's try the back door."

We got around to the back and almost lost some time looking at the grave someone started digging. Wasn't six feet deep, not yet, but a good halfway there. Just lit a fire under us to keep moving.

And that backdoor, wouldn't you just know it opened?

Well, we got that door open and there was Mrs. Dumas, lying in a heap against the mud room floor. Not wearing a stitch more than her bathrobe, and it wasn't doing its job all too well.

Look, I know those priests take all kinds of vows. But I've lived in this world for a few years now, and I don't trust a man's vow any further than I trust the man. And I didn't know that priest enough to trust him with a half-naked unconscious woman.

No, I'm not saying he'd've touched her. But looking at her wrong when she was like that, that was a violation too. Far as I'm concerned.

So I shoved him along on his way before I knelt down to see how bad she was hurt.

It was bad. Concussion, and some half-dozen broken ribs. But you know all that. Medical report's damn near public knowledge now. I'm just saying I didn't know about the hemorrhaging at the time. Did what I could to wrap her chest, but I could tell she needed a hospital, not an old field medic. So after I did what little I could I adjusted her robe and kept moving.

And while I was doing what I could do, that priest was doing what he could do. Before he set foot out of that mudroom he had his crucifix out and was spewing Latin like steam from a boiling teakettle.

He didn't get three steps before he stopped and knelt.

That was when I found the boy, Mason. Throat smashed in just like everybody says. Lots of blood too. But my skills, they didn't have nothing to do with the dead, so I kept moving while the priest said some more prayers. So no, I don't know if he had any other wounds.

Damnedest thing happened then though. Or maybe it was the blessedest thing. I don't know. I just know that I've heard the last rites more times than I'd like. Heard them plenty on the battlefield, and I know something of how the cadence goes.

And I know that priest wasn't half-done when he stopped. Hefted his cross like a weapon, pointing it at the basement stairs. Latin flowing out of him like someone opened his taps all the way.

Now this next thing. This was something I didn't think about at the time. But that doesn't make it any less true. At the time, though, I was just too worried, finding hurt people, to think about a little thing like the temperature.

What you have to understand is that Briar's a pretty warm place in the summertime. And while that June hadn't been special hot, it held its heat pretty far into the night. Had to have been in the 60s when I came running across the street with my bag.

But the inside of that house, it was cold. My daddy would have called it cold as a witch's tit. In the army we called it cold enough to shrivel you, if you take my meaning.

But after the priest spat that Latin at the basement door... I swear to you I'm not making this up, and I'll swear it on a stack of bibles if you like. After he said his piece the air warmed up like the sun coming out from behind the clouds.

No, there was no sun and no clouds. Had to be one in the Ack Emma by then. I just know that the priest aimed his crucifix at the basement door, spat some Latin, and the whole place warmed up.

Well, of course that made the basement my next stop. That was when I found those kids Eli and Dee, babbling and hustling up the stairs like Old Nick himself was on their tail. But they didn't look hurt so I let them pass.

And I found Lex. Abrasions on his hands, and the skin of his face. Nasty, rusty cut on the bottom of his right foot. But those things, those are little. They're not enough to kill a man. And Lex, he was stone dead. His hair was a shock of white, and his eyes were wide as quarters, and his body was stiff like he'd been dead a good long time.

Yeah, I've heard about the M.E.'s report. I'm not saying it makes any sense. But you people are paying me to tell the truth, to tell the story as I know it. And that's what you get.

What else do you want to know?

We got Mrs. Dumas to the hospital just as fast as I could get an ambulance here, and I'm not ashamed to say I called that driver, Gill, directly. I don't go through dispatch, not in Briar. Same reason I called Sheriff Dalton at home to get his end started.

Mrs. Dumas was in that hospital for a good, long time. Her kids stayed with me for the first few days, but she had some family out in Jersey. They were out before the end of the weekend, and they took the kids with them when they left.

No, they didn't go straight home. Not with Gina Dumas in a hospital. They took those kids to a hotel. Told them they didn't have to. I was happy to have the kids stay, but the kids wanted to get just as far from that house as they could. And I don't blame them.

Imagine they wanted to get away from the press, too. Little town like Briar, we get a story like that and there's no way to keep it quiet. It was all blamed on poor Lex, of course, 'cept for the ones who say it was a ghost.

No, I'm not saying Lex was possessed. You'll notice the priest never said that either, and Rome called him back to Italy before Mrs. Dumas was even out of the hospital.

Maybe it was ghosts. Maybe poor Lex Dumas was just a troubled individual. All I do know for certain is that you couldn't pay me enough to spend the night in that house.

But if you're so keen to do it, why don't you buy the place too? I'm sure Gina Dumas would be happy to sell.

CLOSING NOTE

The film crew that interviewed Mr. McElroy in 1996 disappeared shortly thereafter. Only the McElroy Interview indicates that they made any attempt to spend the night in the Dumas' house. Representatives for the Dumas family indicate that the film crew made no official attempts to contact the Dumas family for permission to enter the premises. The Briar Police Department has no record of any calls from that neighborhood around the time of the 1996 interview.

The Dumas family has never spoken on the record about the events that took place during their short tenure in their house in Briar, California, in 1989. All requests for interviews have been declined, and the family's official position is that everything transpired as recorded in the police incident report.

They have declined to comment on the story as relayed in these pages, and they have never spoken publicly about the McElroy Interview.

The Dumas family have confirmed that the property is available for sale, as is.

SIGN UP FOR STEFON'S NEWSLETTER

Stefon loves to keep in touch with his readers, and loves to keep you reading. The best way for him to do both is for you to sign up for his newsletter.

Sign up at http://www.stefonmears.com/join

If you sign up for Stefon's newsletter, you get...

- Monthly updates about his publishing and travel schedules
- His latest news, in brief, and answers to reader questions
- A free short story for signing up
- List-only offers and occasional specials
- Plus a free short story every month!

ABOUT THE AUTHOR

Stefon Mears has been in his share of haunted houses. Stefon has more than thirty books to his credit, and he never stops writing. He earned his M.F.A. in Creative Writing from N.I.L.A., and his B.A. in Religious Studies (double emphasis in Ritual and Mythology) from U.C. Berkeley. He's a lifelong gamer and fantasy fan. Stefon lives in Portland, Oregon, with his wife and three cats.

Look for Stefon online:
www.stefonmears.com
himself@stefonmears.com